Flames in the Jungle

Flames in the Jungle

A Novel

John Cunyus

iUniverse, Inc.
New York Lincoln Shanghai

Flames in the Jungle

Copyright © 2006 by John G. Cunyus

All rights reserved. No part of this book may be used or reproduced by any means, graphic, electronic, or mechanical, including photocopying, recording, taping or by any information storage retrieval system without the written permission of the publisher except in the case of brief quotations embodied in critical articles and reviews.

iUniverse books may be ordered through booksellers or by contacting:

iUniverse
2021 Pine Lake Road, Suite 100
Lincoln, NE 68512
www.iuniverse.com
1-800-Authors (1-800-288-4677)

This is a work of fiction. All of the characters, names, incidents, organizations and dialogue in this novel are either the products of the author's imagination or are used fictitiously.

ISBN-13: 978-0-595-40800-9 (pbk)
ISBN-13: 978-0-595-85164-5 (ebk)
ISBN-10: 0-595-40800-1 (pbk)
ISBN-10: 0-595-85164-9 (ebk)

Printed in the United States of America

To the beautiful women of Colombia, especially Rocio.

The Characters

Hernan Virrey—a Colombian coffee baron and businessman, with mysterious ties to almost everyone who matters in the region.

Jorge Toromillo—a cold-blooded, meticulous intelligence operative working for…whom?

Miguel Escalante—a young man from a modest family who becomes a rising star in the Colombian army.

Ana Restrepo—a beautiful, fearless reporter from the weekly magazine *Pensamiento*.

Don Evans—a reluctant American Foreign Service Officer, thrust into a role he never sought.

The *FARC*—Spanish acronym for the "Revolutionary Armed Forces of Colombia," the larger of the two main guerrilla armies in Colombia.

Ernesto Botero—a graying guerrilla who lives and dies for the communist cause.

Antonio Gonzalez—a Venezuelan spy whose murder helps spark a war.

Jabreel Daniel—an airport guard, in the wrong place at the wrong time.

David Newman—a Southwest airlines Captain who does everything possible to save those in his care.

James Cook—a prominent American congressman caught in the wrong place at the wrong time.

Mariano Perez—President of Venezuela, whose ill-timed words lead to his own undoing.

Vicente Arena—President of the Republic of Colombia, determined to crush a forty-year-old insurgency.

Chapter One

Hernan Virrey sat in an outdoor bar on the old city wall of Cartagena, Colombia, watching the sultry day die in a spectacular sunset over the western Carribean. The continual roar of the city surrounded him: the honking taxis, the clatter of horse drawn carriages, the sounds of vendors and tourists.

The sun painted the massive old Spanish fortress on the opposite hill a fantastic gold, its color reflecting off Virrey's immaculate white satin suit. As he took in the scene, he considered the audacity of the Spaniards who had built it. They conquered this country with a few determined men, he reflected.

"We're going to do the same thing," Virrey said softly to himself, his enthusism building inside.

Then he laughed. "This time the fools won't even know it happened!"

He leaned back on the metal chair, straightening his tie and sipping his manhattan. A sea breeze swept over the wall. He looked back to the centuries-old, colonial cathedral. Then he looked at his watch. Virrey was an anomaly among people who seldom lived by the clock. He was a punctual man. He was also not a man who tolerated being kept waiting.

This time he was having to wait. He scanned the city impatiently, eyes rising up through the smoky sky to La Popa, the white monastery atop the highest hill in town. The Spanish built it for religious and military purposes. Lookouts from there scanned these seas for centuries, watching out for English and Dutch pirates. Now tourists scanned them, at times seeing the stark contrast between the glittering Cartagena of the waterfront hotels and the squalid Cartagena of the refugees, some living at the feet of La Popa itself.

The sunset faded and the lights of the old city blazed on, bathing the ancient monuments in their spectacular colors. Music began to fill the breeze from a half-dozen clubs and street musicians. The waiter asked Virrey if he'd like to order.

"Another manhattan," he snapped.

Virrey's tone made it clear he had no desire to chat with the waiter the way tourists did. The waiter was attuned to the difference between chatty tourists and upper-class Colombian businessmen. He cursed under his breath as he turned away to fetch the drink.

At long last, at least fifteen minutes after Virrey's patience ended, a tall, olive-skinned man with a bushy mustache appeared at the top of the ramp leading to the battlement. Virrey called to him at once.

"Jorge," he barked. "Over here."

The other man, black eyes burning out from under a thick head of hair, came over.

"You're late," Virrey said.

"You're early," the man replied.

If Virrey wasn't one to tolerate waiting, the other man wasn't one to tolerate intolerance.

Virrey recovered himself. He cleared his throat and said, "It's ready on this end. We've brought the teams into Vaupés and arranged things with the police. Is everything set on your end?"

"We're ready," the man answered. "The *FARC* crew is top notch."

"Do they have any…suspicions? The *FARC* boys, I mean," Virrey asked, fishing for the right word.

"No," Jorge answered. "No idea whatsoever."

"Good," Virrey answered, straightening his tie again. "Have a drink."

The waiter brought Virrey his manhattan. "*Y usted?*" he asked the other man.

"Yeah," he answered. "Chivas on the rocks."

"*Si señor,*" the waiter answered.

"In your professional opinion," Virrey asked once the waiter had stepped away, "will the Americans take the bait?"

The other man nodded his head yes. "When they find out about my involvement and investigate my connections, they'll only be able to come to one conclusion."

"Then what?" Virrey asked.

They'd been through this a hundred times before, but he still wanted to hear it.

"Then," the man said, "they'll react like wounded elephants. They'll stomp the shit out of the little bastards they think caused it…just like Afghanistan."

Virrey and the other man sat in silence, soaking in the sights and sounds of the old city along with the humid air. The drink came.

"To Colombia," Virrey said, proposing a toast.

"To *our* Colombia," the other said.

Miguel Escalante woke up at 5:00 a.m., as he always did. He could hear the constant whirring of the insects outside the mosquito net, punctuated by bird song and the occasional cry of an animal. As always in the jungle, it was hot and humid.

Escalante sat up from his sleeping bag, dampened a rag with water from his canteen, and wiped the night sweat from his face. No one else was stirring. He felt around for matches and candle. They were exactly where he left them, as they always were. The tiny bit of remaining moonlight hardly penetrated the jungle canopy. He lit the candle, opened his Bible, and began to read.

Escalante had gotten in the habit of doing that after watching the American movie *Patton* as a nine-year-old boy. In the movie a reporter sees a Bible on General Patton's bed and asks, "General, do you read that book?"

Patton, played by George C. Scott, replied, "Every goddamned day."

He first saw *Patton* the same year his mother died, leaving him and his two younger brothers with his father, who ran a small business in the Kennedy neighborhood of Bogotá. His mother and father had come to the ironically-named neighborhood in Bogotá after the guerrillas overran their tiny mountain village of Santa Elena, in Boyacá, to the north.

Miguel thought back on his childhood in the mountains, a dozen hours by bus away from the capital of Bogotá. It seemed so normal in his childhood to see men farming mountainsides where goats could barely stand. Yet the stark beauty of the land produced little in the way of wealth for its inhabitants. The younger ones almost always left, making their way to one of the big cities. They left behind an increasingly empty countryside, full of old men in traditional fedoras and woolen ponchos and old women in brightly colored skirts.

Three thousand people lived in Santa Elena, at the foot of the *Sierra Nevada de Cocuy* mountain. The town, built of white stone, clustered around a colonial era plaza dominated by the ever-present Catholic church. The sole telephone in town stood on a corner of the plaza. Television didn't arrive until he was seven. It was as common to see a burro trudging up the mountain trails as to see a car.

The town itself was divided by political affiliation. The *conservadores* (Conservatives) lived on one side. The *liberales* (Liberals) lived on the other. By the time Miguel was born there was an uneasy peace between the two groups, but absolutely no love. In the late 1940s, long before his birth, Colombia had splintered between the two parties. Even tiny Santa Elena had been ripped in two. In 1948, at the height of the troubles, the *conservadores* in Santa Elena, with greater numbers, turned on their *liberal* neighbors with a sudden vengeance, hunting them down in the streets, burning their houses, and chasing them up into the mountains.

Even after a generation, the wounds hadn't healed. Many of the exiled *liberales* turned to communism in the 1950s, as Colombia struggled to throw off its dictatorship. When the first post dictatorial government proved incompetent and corrupt, these leftists took to the hills again. It was the heyday of Fidel, Mao, and communist revolutionaries. The guerrilla movements were born.

In Miguel's childhood, the guerrillas had swept back through the mountain towns of northern Boyacá, reinforced by infiltrators coming up from neighboring Arauca province and its steaming, tropical flat lands. With the younger generation gone, the government and army couldn't hold the country. The army pulled back, leaving the guerrillas to avenge themselves on their former right-wing oppressors. It had been brutal and effective.

Miguel's father was a policeman in Santa Elena. The rebels initially left the police alone, preferring not to have to do that job. Their attitude soon changed. The Escalantes learned there was a price on their heads.

Miguel remembered vividly the terror. His father and mother had awakened him and his brothers in the middle of the night. Miguel was nine. The parents crammed the children into the back of a *volquete*, one of the ancient trucks that made the run down the mountains to Tunja, the provincial capital, and Bogotá. They'd stuffed inside the few possessions they could carry, then climbed in themselves. Miguel's great-uncle drove. He wasn't on the guerrilla hit list.

The truck rumbled down the hairpin mountain turns throughout the night. Miguel remembered the jolting and jarring as the old truck's gears ground their way over potholes in the road. Twice, they were hailed to a stop at guerrilla checkpoints.

"What have you got in the truck, old man?" Miguel heard one of the guerrillas say.

His great-uncle, stepping out onto the pavement, pounded the palm of his hand against the side of the truck. The metal resounded like an enormous empty barrel.

"Nothing inside," the great-uncle said. "I'm taking it to Tunja to buy asphalt for the road."

For an agonizing moment, the family inside heard nothing. Did the guard believe him? Would he climb up and look in?

Finally, the guard said, "Okay. Drive on."

At the next checkpoint, the great-uncle told the guards the same story. Then he added, "They let us through south of Santa Elena."

This time the guerrillas waved them through without question.

The family arrived in Bogotá like so many: with little more than the clothes on their back. Miguel's mother died shortly after the family arrived in Bogotá. Though he couldn't articulate it until years later, young Miguel knew from the beginning that the stress of their terrorized flight had killed her.

Don Evans, the new American vice-consul in Cartagena, wasn't fond of the assignment. He'd been in the foreign service twenty years and would have preferred jobs in Europe, the Far East, or stateside. Anywhere, he thought, but Colombia!

Colombia had always scared and baffled him. Bogotá was an American's urban nightmare. And Cartagena was worse. Yet the State Department in Washington kept reassigning him there throughout his career, despite his objections. It seemed like once in Colombia, always in Colombia.

Evans still marveled at how chaotic Colombian life was. In all his years visiting the country, he'd never seen a Colombian stop voluntarily at a stop sign. For Colombians, the lines defining lanes on the streets were mere suggestions. Three and sometimes four cars would contest two official lanes, each driver leaning on his horn and trying to browbeat the others. As often as he'd seen it, it still amazed him to see dilapidated horse-drawn carts cantering down the streets amidst all the careening traffic.

Evans, with his balding brown hair and light mustache, would try in his uncertain way to communicate this strange world each time he came home and talked to people in the States. "In American cities we have one bus company and regular bus stops. In Colombia there are half a dozen companies at least in each city. A bus stop is wherever someone waves down a bus driver."

Evans' first experience of a Colombian street was permanently etched in his memory. He'd been assigned to go to a meeting in Bogotá. He ventured out of the embassy, coming upon an area nearby which served as an unofficial "transit center." Taxis, buses, motorcycles, bicycles, private cars, and the ever-present horse-drawn carts thundered down a nine-lane stretch. Pedestrians braved the riotous traffic, walking out into the center lanes to hail buses and cabs. Cars screeched and swerved to avoid small children selling mangos and papayas to passers-by. He remembered nothing about the meeting, but he never forgot the traffic getting there. They all seemed to be in such a goddamn hurry, he thought, but they never seemed to get where they were going.

Every time he came back to the States, it took him a few days to adjust to people who obeyed traffic signs, yielded right of way, and, in general, were pleasant to each other on the road. He always found himself driving like a Colombian for awhile, until he remembered that people actually did get in trouble with the law in the US for doing such things.

When his American friends complained about how bad things were in their own cities, he just shook his head. "You have no idea," he told them.

Life in the rest of the world in general and Colombia specifically was so different, so alien, the only way to believe it was to experience it.

Needless to say, young Miguel Escalante did not have a high opinion of the guerrillas as he came of age. After finishing high school, he took a step few Colombians of his generation did voluntarily: he enrolled in the *General Jose Maria Cordova Escuela Militar de Cadetes*, the Colombian equivalent of West Point.

Inspired by General Patton, he graduated with honors and became a *Subteniente*, a second lieutenant, in the Colombian army. He didn't do it out of family tradition or a desire to enjoy the rampant corruption. He did it out of love for country and a passionate hatred for the guerrillas.

Several years later, the Colombian army had been humiliated in these same jungles where Escalante now sat reading. The guerrillas overran the departmental capital of Mitú, Vaupés, in an unexpected assault. Miguel was among the officers who led the recapture of the tiny, isolated city, deep in the jungle.

He distinguished himself in the eyes of his superiors by his utter ferocity and fearlessness under fire. In a war where many on both sides refused to fire their weapons, Escalante was merciless. He gunned down the guerrillas whether they stood and fought or not, letting loose a fury that had burned inside him since his mother's death.

Despite his personal valor, the army as a whole could go no further. The guerrillas proceeded to drive them out of a Switzerland-sized chunk of their own country. Mitú was an island of army control in a sea of guerrillas. Like most Colombians, Miguel was fervently patriotic. The army's defeat was a personal insult to him.

Still influenced by *Patton*, his family's trauma, and his nation's humiliation, Miguel Escalante decided to stay in the military. The army would be no temporary activity on the way to other things. His adolescent vow had been to save Colombia's honor. It became his life's work.

Thinking about it now, in the tent, he laughed to himself slightly. Lots of kids make vows. Most of them don't wind up sleeping in the jungle as a result. He understood why the guerrillas would leave steamy Arauca behind and climb up to the coolness of Boyacá and its mountains. There were days he wished he could do the same.

He knew that wasn't going to happen anytime soon. He learned to stifle his own desires, like a good soldier. The romantic, bookish, patriotic teenager had become an intense, disciplined man. His hatred of those who had killed his mother was unrelenting.

The long-formed habit of daily Bible reading set him apart from practically everyone else he knew. His favorite book was Joshua, because

Joshua had utterly destroyed the enemies of his country. Another passage had burned itself into his mind as well: "Shake out your sleeves lest they hold a bribe!"

As a result, Miguel Escalante had developed two qualities sorely lacking in Colombian military life. He was ruthlessly self-disciplined. He was also incorruptible. Those around him jokingly called him "San Miguel." Those who knew him better called him "Joshua." It was, in fact, his life's ambition to utterly destroy Colombia's insurgent enemies.

Chapter Two

Ana Restrepo stood up from her desk in the office at *Pensamiento* ("Thought"), a weekly Colombian news magazine that gained notoriety of late by exposing links between the National Police and the *FARC* guerrillas. It was a dangerous business. Both parties were well-armed and vengeful. Journalists in Colombia had a long history of turning up dead when their stories stepped on such toes.

Ana had good reason to be wary. She had blown the lid off a recent scandal involving a fat National Police General. The General had been working with supposedly demobilized *paras* in the police force to kidnap well-off Colombians and foreigners and sell them to the *FARC*. For years, he'd managed to keep investigators and reporters at bay. Ana, though, had gotten to him.

She found she "got to" a lot of people that way. In a country famous for beautiful women, she was among the most beautiful, with her light brown skin, green eyes, dark hair, and exquisite figure. Her sense of style was restrained, yet elegant. Ana discovered early on in life that her mere presence seemed to disorient the males around her. When she flashed them her beautiful smile as well, the effect was almost breathtaking. She learned to use this beauty like a weapon.

Like Miguel Escalante, she had grown up in an era of violence and national humiliation. Though her family circumstances were much more prosperous than Miguel's, she too was a fervent patriot, hating the fact that even the other Latin countries referred to Colombia as "*Locombia*," the "crazy country." She decided in her university days to use the gifts she'd been given to the benefit of her country.

When she'd come into her editor's office not long ago with a detailed, incriminating tape of the General of the National Police bragging about how much he'd made selling a recently-kidnaped German businessman to the *FARC*, the editor had blurted out incredulously, "How did you get him to say this?"

"Don't ask," Ana told him.

Parts of her job were distasteful. She wouldn't tell the world about them. But they were just that—parts of her job, part of her determination to help her country.

The reality was Ana had seduced the man. They'd met for drinks in a downtown bar, Ana pretending to an interest she absolutely didn't have. After a few drinks, the man had put his fat hand on Ana's slim thigh, leaning ever closer. She didn't push him away.

"I know what you want," he slurred drunkenly to her. "You want to get me drunk and seduce me. Then you want me to tell you about the goddamn German we sold to the *FARC!* You reporters are all the same. You must think we're idiots!"

As a matter of fact, she did think he was an idiot. But this idiot was already under her spell. Ana quietly switched on her tape recorder as the General got drunker. As always, she discretely poured her own drinks out. After a couple of hours, the drunken General insisted they leave together. Ana went with him, holding him up as he staggered out into the street. They'd gone to his apartment.

Ana was prepared. Her body was her weapon. She always carried a small vial of rohypnol, the date rape drug, in her hand bag. When one of her drunken fools wanted to go too far, she found it worked just as well on men as it did on women.

Ana and the General sat down together on the sofa. The General's female employee brought them coffee. He roared at the girl, "Coffee, hell no! Bring us martinis!"

The girl hurried out to fix the drinks. The General pawed at Ana's breasts through her green silk blouse, his sodden breath hot against her neck. He was fumbling with the buttons on her blouse when the girl came back with the drinks.

The girl put them down and left the room. While he was distracted, Ana hid the vial of rohypnol in one hand. The General unbuttoned the rest of her blouse, then ran his hand inside her bra, fondling her gorgeous breast. She silently cracked open the vial and dumped it in his drink while he was preoccupied.

"I'm a little thirsty," she said

The General reached over and got the drinks. She carefully picked up hers and pretended to sip it. He took a great drunken gulp of his, exhaling sharply as the gin burned the roof of his mouth. He put the drink down and turned back to Ana's beautiful breasts, bending over to take her nipple in his mouth.

In a moment, though, the drug combined with the alcohol began to work. She felt his drool running down her nipple and onto her stomach. He sat up suddenly, a quizzical look in his eyes, then slumped over backwards. The fat fool had passed out.

Ana put a pillow under his head. She wiped the spit off her breast with a blanket lying nearby, then covered the General with the blanket. She got up, rearranged her blouse, let herself out, and took a taxi home. After an hour-long shower to try and wipe every last sensation of the fool's hand and tongue from her body, she dried off, dressed, and took the tape to her editor.

It was distasteful, even to her. But now the General was in prison, his kidnaping ring had been smashed, and Ana Restrepo had to have a bodyguard every time she left the building.

Miguel Escalante's first years in the army were tough for him and for the nation. The corruption and ineptitude that surrounded him almost drove him out. How could an army win a war when its commanders regularly brutalized civilians and let guerrillas walk out of traps if the bribe was enough? How could it even fight when its politicians gave away the national territory to the very enemies seeking to destroy them?

Instead of spurring peace talks, it spurred only spiraling violence and kidnaping. At the same time, ruthless land barons and drug lords began forming their own militias, the *paramilitarios*, to defend their interests. The *paras* were as violent and lawless as the guerrillas. The civil war essentially triangulated, with guerrillas and *paras* fighting each other as well as the Colombian army.

Deep down, Escalante had faith that someday his country would come to share his revulsion. It had. A string of concessions to the guerrillas resulted finally in granting them an official sanctuary in the zone they had "liberated" from the army. The backlash began when Colombians, fed up with the endless cycle of violence, elected a President who was serious about crushing the insurgency. "We talked and talked to them," said President-elect Vicente Arena, whose own father had been kidnaped and murdered by the guerrillas. "It gained us nothing but blood and kidnaping. Now we will crush them."

At first people laughed, not least the guerrillas and the *paras*. But Arena approached this with a determination and honesty few others had. Within a few years, he negotiated the demobilization of the *paras* and actually managed to unleash the army against the rebels.

Escalante chuckled to himself again in the candlelight. The thought of "unleashing the army" would have been a joke when he'd first joined. Back then the army was fresh-faced conscripts and corrupt officers. Now it was deadly serious. He himself was one of the reasons the army was a force to be reckoned with.

Ana found most Colombian men far too *machista*, too patronizing, too willing to take without giving. Miguel Escalante was different from the first. She'd interviewed him after hearing stories of his bravery in Mitú. Every army needs a hero and Miguel was being groomed for the role.

She brought her usual skepticism to the meeting, which took place in a simple office in an army barracks on the edge of Bogotá. Miguel, though, had taken her completely by surprise. She was accustomed to a world where no one was quite what they seemed, where everyone had a hidden agenda. But he struck her as completely sincere and straightforward. It didn't hurt that he was both handsome and, almost as appealing, completely unaware that he was.

She invited him to dinner, almost impulsively, after the interview. Surprised by her straightforwardness, he agreed. They ate and talked for two hours. Ana had a glass of wine. Miguel, she noticed, drank only water. Afterwards he took her back to her apartment and walked her up the steps. She intended to invite him in, but before she could he thanked her for the evening, shook her hand, and left.

Ana couldn't get him out of her mind all week. Did he actually reject her? Was there a girlfriend she didn't know about? Having a man turn away from her at the door was a completely new experience.

She did a little journalistic background on him, supposedly to write a better story. She was actually trying to find out who her competition was. Thoughts of Miguel filled her mind, making her feel disoriented, a little dizzy.

Wednesday the next week she called him again, asking for a followup interview. Miguel agreed and they met over dinner. This time they talked for hours, lost in each other's company.

"Miguel," she said, "would you like to go for a…a walk?"

It was all she could think of. Anything, anything, she thought, to keep the evening from ending!

He nodded yes. They paid the check and stepped out into the cool Bogotá night, walking up the sidewalk. The lights flickered up the side of the mountain. She honestly thought she would fall over, her feelings were so intense.

She stumbled a little. Miguel reached out and took her arm.

"Are you okay?" he asked.

"Yes. Just a little trip," she said.

She kept hold of his arm, reaching down to take his hand in hers. In the instant of doing so, every possible anxiety flashed through her head. Will he let go? Will he…

He didn't. She felt his strong, soldier's hand envelop hers. This time her knees really were shaking. They must have walked for two hours, completely oblivious to the passage of time. Miguel finally looked at his watched and said, "Oh no! I'm so sorry…I have a meeting to go to."

He hailed a cab. They got in together and rode in silence, hand in hand, to her apartment. He walked her up the steps again. Their eyes met at the top. Ana closed hers, expecting a kiss. Instead, the taxi honked on the street for Miguel.

He took her hand, looked into her eye, and said, "I've had an incredible time with you."

She squeezed his hand as lovingly as she could. He let go, reluctantly, turned toward the street and…left.

Two days later, he called her. By this time she knew exactly what she was feeling. She was head over heels, swimmingly, wildly in love. Her heart leapt when she heard his voice on the phone. It made her almost dizzy to think he might have some of the same feelings as well.

"Would you…would you like to have dinner?" he asked, uncertainly.

"Yes!" Ana said, then felt embarrassed by how enthusiastically she'd said it. "Yes, of course," she repeated, trying to sound calmer. "Tonight?"

"Yes," Miguel said. "Tonight."

The two met in a small restaurant not far from Ana's office. This time both of them drank a glass of wine. After dinner, they walked again, lost to everything else.

"Would you..." Ana began to ask uncertainly.

"Would I what?" Miguel responded.

"Would you...like to come back to my apartment?" she said.

She'd never had to ask before.

Miguel blushed slightly and said yes. The two walked to her apartment. Ana found herself dreading the steps leading to the door. Would he stop at the top and leave again, she wondered?

He didn't. She unlocked the door, turned off the security system her editor had installed, and the two went in.

"Would you...uh...like something to drink?" she asked.

"A glass of water," he answered. "First, though, may I..."

He didn't finish the sentence.

"Yes?" she asked.

"May I use your restroom?" he asked sheepishly.

They both laughed, breaking the tension.

"Of course, silly," she said, pointing the way.

Ana poured him a glass of water, then sat on the couch waiting. No rohypnol necessary this time, she thought to herself.

He came out and sat beside her. They joined hands, making nervous small talk. She felt like she would explode inside.

"Miguel," she said, turning to him.

He turned and looked into her eyes. It looked like they were on fire. She put her arms around him and pulled him to her, kissing him deeply, profoundly. When she felt him kissing back, she almost melted. She pulled him down off of the couch onto the carpeted floor, the two intertwining together.

Then, out of breath, Ana began to undress. She unbuttoned her blouse, letting it slip to the floor. Miguel watched her silently.

"Do you mind?" she asked in a hoarse whisper.

Her heart almost died at the thought that he might mind. Miguel said nothing.

She unclasped her skirt, letting it fall as well. She knelt there before him, wearing only her black lace bra and panties. She reached behind and unclasped the bra, letting it, too, fall to the floor.

Miguel sighed deeply at the sight of her smooth skin and beautiful breasts. She wasn't sure what his sigh meant. Oh God, she thought, what if he leaves? What if I offended him? She couldn't hold back, though.

She stood up and slipped her panties off, standing before him completely naked. He stood up too, unsure. She had never felt as naked in her entire life, absolutely vulnerable before another person.

She caught his hand and brought it to her breast. He caressed her tentatively.

"Ana," he whispered.

She almost couldn't answer, so afraid of what he might say. She finally managed to say, "Yes, Miguel."

"I…I've never done this before," he said.

"Oh, my love!" she sighed, relieved beyond words. He wasn't rejecting her! "I'll show you everything!"

Chapter Three

Two weeks later Miguel was back in the jungle, hunting the guerrillas. Ana, in Bogotá, was so in love with him she could hardly breathe. Yet she still had a job to do.

As part of doing that job, she agreed to have lunch with a smitten admirer from the Venezuelan Embassy. She had no interest in him whatsoever personally. Truth be told, she found him as repulsive as she'd found the General, especially now when her mind was full of Miguel Escalante. But tensions between Venezuela and Colombia had been high enough in recent years to make this a potentially valuable professional relationship. It too might become a case of "Don't ask," if an editor ever wanted to know how she came by her information.

Ana left her office quickly enough that the bodyguard had to run to catch up. They stepped out onto a teeming street, a few blocks north of the *Plaza de Bolivar*, center of Colombia's political life. Ana turned south, walking a couple of blocks down to the corner fronting the massive national cathedral. Then she turned west, climbing the cobbled street into the ancient Candelaria district to meet Ivan Marez, the man from the Venezuelan Embassy.

Marez was waiting for her in front of the restaurant. He kissed her solicitously on both cheeks and they went inside. He was only a few years older than her, but his lifestyle was already beginning to tell. He was heavy, just at the point of being fat. He oozed self-importance in his pen-striped navy suit and bright red tie, a tiny Venezuelan flag pinned to his lapel. It made him feel even more important to have a woman like Ana accompanying him to lunch.

Marez made small talk and Ana politely played along. The themes were almost always the same. Marez talked about Marez, whatever else he seemed to be saying. Relations between Colombia and Venezuela all had to do with Marez. Venezuela's President Mariano Perez, so good at baiting the Americans and meddling in Latin politics, was also all about Marez. Ana found it tedious, but the information behind it was…well…useful. Marez himself never noticed how Ana felt.

This time he was laboring on about how the Venezuelan President was going to insult the American Secretary of State in response to a speech she had made. It was his idea, Marez insisted. "I told the Ambassador that Perez should tell that black bitch in Washington to be careful."

It appalled Ana that Marez should insult both the race and gender of the American Secretary of State. It wasn't a leap in logic to assume that if he spoke this way about one woman he probably spoke that way about all women, however accomplished they might be. She shuddered involuntarily at the thought of this unpleasant man talking behind her back.

"Don't you think you should be a little more…diplomatic?" she asked, fishing around for the word. "After all, she is the American Secretary of State and you are a diplomat."

She played along with Marez's fantasy that insulting the Secretary of State was his idea. Marez laughed contemptuously. "Of course not," he blustered. "What will the gringos do? I told Perez to tell her 'Don't mess with me, Madam. I bite!'"

Ana noticed the way Marez was building the whole thing up in his own mind. It was no longer a matter of simply suggesting it to the Ambassador. Marez convinced himself he had told President Perez personally. Still, the fact that a second-level Venezuelan diplomat in Bogotá should express such disdain for the Americans in the person of their Secretary of State struck Ana as newsworthy.

Marez, for all his bluster, was not a fool. He said, did, and felt exactly what his masters at the Embassy and in the Foreign Ministry in Caracas, the Venezuelan capital, were saying. If he spoke derisively of the Americans, that must be the tune in the Foreign Ministry as well. He's playing it right down to the last note, Ana thought to herself.

Sure enough, when Ana got back to the office CNN and the BBC were both airing the story of President Perez insulting the American Secretary of State. The Secretary had urged him publicly a few days earlier not to meddle in the affairs of other Latin American countries. In a speech today in Caracas addressed to her Perez said, "Do not mess with me, Madam Secretary. I bite!"

Marez may be a complete boor, Ana thought, but he's a good source. In her story in the following week's edition, Ana said something to the effect that the Venezuelan President's remarks were being echoed faithfully by his diplomats in Bogotá. She cleaned up the language. Marez called to chide her light-heartedly about using his words but not his name. He also clipped the article and sent it to the Foreign Ministry in Caracas, just to be sure they knew he was following their lead.

Chapter Four

Ernesto Botero had long since decided he was too old for this shit. He also realized that deciding so didn't matter. Joining the *FARC* was like joining the mafia: the only ways out were death or victory.

Botero's radical pedigree was solid. His father had been murdered in the 1940s by a right-wing death squad. Ernesto was two years old. His uncle, a Jesuit professor in Medellin, took in the traumatized little boy. Years later, radicalized by the brutality of the ruling elites around him, eyes opened by his uncle's Marxist scholarship, Botero had gone to the hills to fight for what he believed.

In the early years, now so far removed in time they seemed even to him like a black-and white movie, he believed victory was possible. He was half a generation younger than the heros of the movement, Che and Fidel. Fidel had won in Cuba, hadn't he? But the war had worn on and on.

The imperialists had learned from their loss in Cuba and had determined not to repeat it. The Americans never came in person, the way they did in Vietnam. They didn't have to. Colombia was closer. Their money and power always propped up the fools in Bogotá.

Botero's youthful energy faded with time, but his sense of outrage hadn't. In the early 1980s, as a hardened, middle-aged guerrilla leader, he had personally gone to Bogotá undercover to work in organizing. He'd seen again the same horrible conditions that had driven him to arms as an idealistic youth.

The most vivid was the *Rio Bogotá,* a river running through the heart of the poorest sections of the city. By any stretch it was one of the foulest waterways on earth. From half a mile away you could smell the stench of raw sewage. When the wind blew the wrong way, it was almost unbearable. What could you expect, though, when nearly seven million people crowded into an infrastructure built for a tenth that many?

The worst of it was up close. There, in the flood plain of the river, Colombia's poorest had built their shacks. There they raised their children. Every time it rained a river literally of shit filled their houses. But they had nowhere else to go.

When he'd seen it up close, he felt a violent outrage that affirmed his life's decision. Any government, any system, that allowed some to live in high rises and drive BMWs while others lived in the filth that drained from their toilets was an offense to all that was decent. Botero didn't worry that the *FARC*'s guerrilla war had pushed most of those refugees into the river bed. Real change often required huge costs, but in his opinion the end justified the means.

Ernesto had been to Cuba many times. He knew it was no paradise. He knew the fools on the streets would vote Fidel out if they had the chance. But the fools on the street were ignorant brutes and always had been. In Cuba people didn't live in other peoples' shit. They may not have been rich. They may not have gotten fat. A lot of them may have wanted to leave. But nobody starved in Cuba. What a shame they didn't realize that for the blessing it was.

Behind the *FARCs* lines everyone ate, even if they didn't eat well. Yet the movement had long lost any real chance for victory. Its popular support hovered in low single digits, especially once it had gotten in bed with the drug dealers to fund its battle.

When that alliance steadily brought more American power to bear against it, it had turned to kidnaping. If the rich bastards in the cities wouldn't give even a little to the people living in their shit, they could be made to experience that life themselves. Rich people buying their way out of the *FARC*'s custody now funded most of the battle. Kidnaping, Botero said, was socialist education for the imperialist class.

A man in his sixties, he knew he wouldn't live to see victory. The tide had turned too far against them. The Eastern dominos had fallen, then the Soviet Union itself. China had become a freak of nature: a communist bureaucracy riding herd on a capitalist explosion. Only Fidel was left. Fidel, Cuba, and the *FARC*. History had its ebbs and flows though. Botero was certain that the tide would flow back in the direction of those who wanted to level the field for all, just as it had flowed away. If the movement had lost its way, it would recover.

Botero had experienced prosperity as well as hardship. He had been part of the leadership when the cadres had taken Mitú and driven the Colombian army from Vaupés. In those heady days it seemed like anything was possible. A succession of incompetent and breathtakingly corrupt Colombian Presidents almost brought about the victory Botero and his comrades couldn't win in the field.

The country very nearly fragmented. The big landowners and capitalist elite organized their own armies, the *paras*. At the height of the guerrilla tide the arrogant fools in Bogotá controlled less than 40 percent of their own country.

Botero admitted to himself the backlash had been as harsh as it was unexpected. This madman, Arena, had been elected six years before, talking about "unleashing the army." Botero and others laughed at him, as did most Colombians. Fresh-faced boys in uniforms were no match for the hardened fighters of the *FARC*.

But Arena had accomplished things no one thought he could. He coopted the *paras*, struck deals with the richest of the rich, and consolidated his war. He used American money and training to transform Colombia's fresh-faced boys into hardened soldiers. He purged the most corrupt of the army's leaders, replacing them with religious zealots who couldn't be bought. And then he sent them up into the hills and down into the jungles to battle the *FARC* where it lived.

The *FARC* leadership had taken Arena's offensive in stride at first. The army might be able to roll up some outer positions and retake some insignificant villages. But the strongholds were just that: strongholds, like Cartagena of old. Once the army began forcing its way into some of these, though, the reality of the situation began to sink in.

Six years of relentless warfare changed the equation. Now the fresh-faced boys (and, increasingly, girls) weren't in the army. Instead, they were the teenagers from destitute towns and villages forced into the *FARC* as their only resort in life. More and more of the country had slipped from the cadre's hands, into the control of the swelling Colombian police state.

Men like Botero were in the cross-hairs. They had once hunted the wealthy and powerful of Colombian society. Now they themselves were the hunted. It did not make Botero sleep any better knowing that his life depended on the kind of forced conscripts manning the front lines.

Even in Vaupés, in the heart of the jungle, the army was making its presence felt. As Botero rose to take his morning coffee, he felt more and more like a man with a noose around his neck, waiting for the trap door to spring open. He'd long since made up his mind, though. He may be too old for all this shit, but he was also too old to surrender.

Chapter Five

The phone rang early Saturday morning in Antonio Gonzalez's high-rise condo on Turtle Creek, one of Dallas' most exclusive neighborhoods. His wife answered it half-asleep, then woke him up. Gonzalez was pissed. "Who would call at this ridiculous hour on a Saturday morning?" he groused, last night's rum banging around in his head like a spike.

"Gonzalez," the voice said.

Gonzalez recognized it at once. "*Don* Jorge," he answered in surprise.

He swallowed his anger quickly. "Why do you do me the…honor…of calling me so early on a Saturday?"

Toromillo calmly ordered Gonzalez to dress and meet him at the office. "But *Don* Jorge," Gonzalez pleaded, "it's Saturday? Can't this wait til Monday?"

Toromillo response left no doubt it couldn't. Gonzalez put down the phone and climbed out of bed. "What now?" his wife said.

"I have to go to the office," he grumbled.

"On a Saturday morning at…," she looked around for the alarm clock. "At 6:30, for God's sake?"

"At 6:30, for God's sake!" he answered. "What do you expect me to do—say no to him?"

He was just as aggravated as she was.

His wife knew immediately who "he" was on the other end of the line. She had never met this shadowy figure whose phone calls ran so much of her husband's life. Gonzalez never told her the man's full name. She only knew that cooperating with him was not voluntary. When the stranger said jump, her husband could only answer how high.

Gonzalez ran a comb through his hair, washed his face, brushed his teeth and got dressed. No tie this morning. If Toromillo wanted him, he'd have to taken him with an open collar.

Minutes after the call, Gonzalez was slipping into the crushed velvet interior of his light blue Mercedes. Ah, he thought, this car is fun to drive even when I'd rather be in bed.

He eased the car down Turtle Creek, past the trendy high rises, then turned down Cole Avenue. Very little was stirring this morning in the elegant restaurants and clubs that had been so vibrant only a few hours before. Gonzalez swung the car onto the service road at Woodall Rogers Freeway, which divided uptown from downtown Dallas, then followed the Freeway west to Field Street. He turned down Field into downtown, pulling into the parking garage at the green, angled skyscraper named Fountain Place, where he had his office.

The attendant on duty was surprised to see him. "You're sure out early, Mr. Gonzalez," the man said.

"Yes, Willie," he answered. "Some things can't wait."

Why they couldn't was an issue he intended to take up with Toromillo.

Gonzalez ostensibly worked for *Petroleos de Venezuela*, PDV, the giant, state-owned Venezuelan oil company, overseeing the company's gas stations in the southwestern United States. In fact, for several years he had been running an industrial espionage operation guided by the Venezuelan secret police. Toromillo was his handler.

Venezuelan President Mariano Perez made no secret of his contempt for the gringos. They needed his oil, he figured, and would buy it one way or another. What Perez hadn't counted on was the toll confronting the Americans had taken on PDV, the oil company that was his regime's and his country's lifeline. In effect, the US government had said, 'Fine, you hate us and want to screw our oil operators in your country. Develop your own spare parts to keep your fields pumping.'

That had proven to be a huge problem. First of all, most of the experienced leaders in the company had been purged by the Perez regime or simply quit. Secondly, Venezuela's crude oil was particularly heavy and difficult to produce. Third, the fields were, in general, old. Keeping up production was capital intensive, especially in terms of intellectual capital, know-how.

Venezuela lacked the know-how on its own. Since American know-how was suddenly hard to come by, the Venezuelan government had kicked its espionage program into high gear. If the Americans wouldn't sell what was needed, the Venezuelans would steal it.

Toromillo, the ruthless, shady bastard from…Gonzalez admitted he didn't exactly know where Toromillo came from. Toromillo was the one who coordinated the stealing. Gonzalez realized he knew little about the man other than his name and the mounds of cash Toromillo supplied to Gonzalez and his spying teams.

Gonzalez despised Toromillo. He wasn't thrilled by the government in Caracas either, though he had more than enough sense to keep his reservations to himself. But he loved the lifestyle the additional cash bought him. Dallas was comfortable, clean, luxurious, a world away from the honking chaos of Caracas or the stifling heat of Maracaibo, the center of Venezuela's oil production.

Stealing the secrets was the easy part. American oil people, mostly from Texas and Oklahoma, were remarkably open and friendly. When Gonzalez asked questions, when his staff took pictures, most oil-patch Americans bent over backwards to accommodate them. These Americans had no idea what was going on in Venezuela, nor did they care. Stealing information from them was like stealing candy from a baby. Usually, though, Toromillo waited until working hours to give assignments.

Gonzalez rode the elevator up to his office. He fiddled around for the key and let himself in. Of course, there was no coffee this morning. Nor was there anyone to make it for him. He grumpily sat at his desk, doing without.

Toromillo liked to keep people waiting. Gonzalez sat at his desk until nearly nine, after being roused so early. He was furious by the time the dark-eyed man came through his office door. As he had on the phone, though, he swallowed the anger. Toromillo scared him.

"*Don* Jorge," Gonzalez said, "what is so important on a Saturday morning? I've waited here two hours?"

"Haven't you heard?" Toromillo said. "Venezuela is going to war with the United States."

Gonzalez gulped in disbelief. "*Don* Jorge is joking, of course."

"Not at all," Toromillo answered with a smile. "*El Presidente* has decided to wring the neck of the American chicken."

"No, no, no," Gonzalez answered. "This is of course one of *Don* Jorge's famous *chistes* (jokes)."

Gonzalez was getting nervous. Where was this going?

"Actually," Toromillo added, "the gringos are going to war with us. They don't know it yet, but they are."

"What you're saying makes no sense, *Don* Jorge," Gonzalez pleaded. "We can't go to war with the gringos, whoever starts it. It would be…" He fumbled for the word. "It would be suicidal if it's serious!."

"You're right," Toromillo agreed. "Madness."

"Then surely we can change the subject to something more real," Gonzalez added.

"Ah, sometimes madness takes hold of the human heart," Toromillo added, his voice little more than a sinister whisper.

"Do you know who the first casualty of our little war is going to be?" Toromillo added.

"No, *Don* Jorge. I can't imagine."

Gonzalez felt a cold fear knifing down his back.

"You, Gonzalez," Toromillo said with a smile. "All that spying…it has to stop."

"B…but you ordered it," Gonzalez complained.

"Unfair," Toromillo agreed, shaking his head. "It is completely unfair."

His voice dripped with sarcasm.

With that, Toromillo pulled a pistol with a silencer from his jacket.

"No, no! I have children!" Gonzalez cried frantically. "Why?"

Two light thuds resounded through the room as the bullets smashed into Gonzalez's sternum. The momentum threw his chair over backwards. He sprawled on the floor, eyes wide open with shock, blood gathering in a pool beneath him. By the time Toromillo put the gun away and walked from the room, Gonzalez's open eyes were lifeless, staring wide and seeing nothing.

The murder of a prominent Venezuelan businessman in his plush downtown office was headline news on the Dallas television stations as well as in the *Dallas Morning News*, Dallas' only surviving daily newspaper. The puzzling part was that the assailant managed to enter and leave the building entirely without a trace. Dallas police performed routine ballistics on the bullets: hollowed out rounds designed to do maximum damage on entry. Nothing extraordinary about either the caliber or the ammunition, other than that.

The Police interviewed the grieving widow, as did the local television stations. "We just don't understand why anyone would do this," she wept into the camera.

Of course, she knew exactly who had done it, even if she didn't know his name. She was too afraid of him to say anything to the police, though. The Venezuelan government made a few comments about the lawlessness of life in the United States, then flew Gonzalez's body and family back to Caracas for the funeral.

The day after the murder, using an untraceable cell phone, Toromillo called Virrey in Cartagena. "Gonzalez is dead," he told him. "Better start making me look like a killer."

"Which, of course, you are," Virrey added.

Both men laughed.

Chapter Six

The phone rang early in Don Evans' office in Cartagena. It had been a typical morning getting to work. Evans, still leery of driving in the port city's lunatic traffic, hopped a ride with a friend in the consulate. They parked under the building as they did every morning, an additional measure of security that helped only when the power was on.

It wasn't this morning. Evans and the friend had to circle up out of the parking basement and onto the street to enter the office. The usual throng of vendors lined the sidewalk, selling everything tourists might or might not need: sunglasses, sun block, bottled drinks, tee-shirts, and beads, always beads. Evans wondered what else might be for sale, if someone only asked.

They stepped over the sleeping body of a derelict on the sidewalk and then up the stairs to the building door. The smell of the ocean two blocks away bathed everything as the sun began to heat things up. As was the case in just about every major street in downtown Cartagena, the police presence was heavy.

Evans looked around and counted up. National, Tourist, and *Vigilancia* police were all represented on the sidewalk. None looked to be over the age of 18, but all were there. Around the corner the Colombian army had its own outpost, with troops drawn from the installation a few blocks away. The soldiers didn't look like boys, he thought.

Once you got used to the sight of men in uniforms carrying submachine guns, he thought, it was almost comforting. If the guerrillas actually attacked downtown Cartagena, though, he wondered if the police would just wind up shooting each other. The consulate had its own cops too, in addition to all the official cops.

The ever-present *Seguridad Privada*, or private security, provided the final layer. This morning the *Seguridad Privada* guard seized his opportunity to talk to the Americans. They usually didn't come out on the street, so he usually didn't even see them. "Señor," he said, "you are American, no?"

Evans nodded warily.

"Please tell people of America Colombia is not about drugs," the man said.

It was a theme Evans heard again and again. Colombians were obsessed with their country's image overseas, especially when it came to the gringos. Much as they made a show of disliking the United States, it mattered a great deal to them what Americans thought.

"Yes, yes, I'll tell them," Evans answered.

Evans entered the building. It was hot. The power had been out in this part of town for quite awhile, apparently. He climbed the stairs inside to the consulate offices on the second floor.

He was already sweating in the humidity when he opened the door. He walked behind the counter and down the hall to his office, stopping at the refrigerator to get a bottle of water. Evans opened the refrigerator door. It was hot in there too.

"Good morning, Mr. Evans," the secretary said.

"Good morning, Jane. Any messages?"

"Yes," she replied. "A Mr. Hernan Virrey called for you. He said it was very important."

"Isn't it always," Evans replied.

He intended it as a joke, but his exasperation was showing.

Jane put on a brave face. "It always seems to be," she said.

"Do we know who he is?" Evans wondered. "Is it worth calling him back?"

"Oh yes, Mr. Evans. We've known Mr. Virrey for years. He's a very big landowner in Quindía Province."

"Then what the hell is he doing in this heat," Evans wondered out loud.

Quindía Province was one of the most pleasant places in the country, the center of Colombia's coffee industry.

"He has a condo on the beach," Jane replied. "Brings his family down. I'd make a point of calling him back."

Jane had been in the consulate quite awhile. As in most offices, it was the administrative staff that held the place together.

Evans sat down behind his desk. The sun was rising over the building across the street, shining directly onto his desk and chair. He closed the shade, but without power it made little difference. Finally, swearing quietly, he lifted the shade and opened the window. At least there was a little air movement. Damn, stinking hot, miserable place, he thought to himself.

He looked down at the stacks of paper on his desk. "They hate us, but they all want to come visit." He was mumbling under his breath.

"Did you say something, Mr. Evans?" Jane called from the outer office.

"Huh? Oh…no, thank you," Evans replied. "Just talking to myself. Anybody say anything about when the power would be back on?"

"They said in half an hour," she answered.

"And when did they say that?" he asked.

"A couple of hours ago."

"It figures," he said.

Maybe it wasn't too late to get a transfer, to change careers, to find some place where it wasn't stifling hot year round, he thought.

Amid the stacks of paper he found the message from Virrey. What the hell, he thought. Maybe it'll be a distraction.

He tapped out the numbers and listened to the odd BEEP-pause-BEEP of Colombia's ancient phone system. A pleasant Spanish-speaking voice picked up on the other end. Evans explained, in English, who he was and why he was calling. The voice said, "One moment, Señor."

"Mr. Evans," the male voice exclaimed when it came on.

It was an enthusiastic greeting.

"Yes, this is Evans. Is this Hernan Virrey?"

"Si señor," he replied. "I mean, yes sir." Virrey chuckled.

"What can I do for you, Mr. Virrey?"

Evans shared none of Virrey's enthusiasm

"Mr. Evans," Virrey said, suddenly serious, "I'm afraid I must see you today."

Evans was a bit perturbed. "Well, you can call my assistant and make an appointment."

"No, Mr. Evans," Virrey replied. "I must see you personally. It is very important."

"What's this about?" Evans answered impatiently, at the point of brushing Virrey off all together? "I've got a day full of meetings and paper work…"

"It concerns a murder," Virrey said. "In Dallas."

When Evans gave no response, Virrey added, "Dallas, Texas."

"Yes," Evans answered impatiently, "I'm familiar with Dallas. You said a murder? Whose murder?"

Evans was growing more impatient. What the hell did a murder in Dallas have to do with him in Cartagena. Dallas had at least two hundred of them each year.

"Haven't you heard?" Virrey asked.

"Heard what?"

"A prominent Venezuelan businessman, an employee of the state oil company, was killed in his office two days ago," Virrey said. "We believe it has to do with an operational plan in the Venezuelan intelligence service."

"Really!" Evans blurted out.

He felt stupid as soon as he said it. "Well, I mean, why do you want to talk to me about it," he asked, trying to recover.

"Mr. Evans," he said, "surely you prefer to hear such things somewhere other than on the telephone."

Again Evans felt stupid. "Well, I guess," he said. "What's your plan?"

All sorts of paranoid thoughts began racing through Evans' head: set up, kidnap, ransom. Before he could check the momentum, his thoughts had him tied to a pole in the Colombian jungle. He shook his head to clear the cobwebs.

"Meet me in front of the Convention Center in twenty minutes," Virrey said. "I will explain everything."

The Convention Center was five minutes away. Evans agreed, figuring it gave him time to find out what the hell was really going on. Besides, Colombians were always late.

Evans walked down the hall and knocked on the Consul-General's door. The Consul-General was his boss.

"He's not there," Jane sang out. "Remember? He's in Barranquilla this week."

"Shit," Evans mumbled to himself.

"I'm sorry," Jane said. "Did you say something?"

"Oh, uh, no," he said. "Have you heard anything about a…a murder in Dallas?" he asked.

"Yes," she replied. "It was on the news last night. An official with PDV, I believe they said."

"PDV?" Evans asked.

"*Petroleos de Venezuela*," Jane said lightly. "It's the state-owned oil company."

"My God," Evans mumbled. "Does this guy think I did it?"

"I'm sorry, Mr. Evans," Jane said. "What did you say?"

"Virrey says he has something to tell me about the murder," Evans said.

Jane immediately rushed to where he stood, by the Consul-General's closed door. "Mr. Evans, you must never say such things out loud here," she scolded. "I'll get security to follow you."

The cold, matter-of-fact way she said it made Evans even more nervous. At that moment the power came out with a jolt. Both of them jumped, though Evans jumped a lot higher than Jane.

Toromillo bought the house on Marsalis Street, a few miles North of Laureland Cemetery in the gritty Oak Cliff neighborhood of Dallas. It backed up on a creek with a huge encircling fence. Given the ethnic mix of the neighborhood, the number of Latino males going in and out would draw no attention.

Gunfire was a common neighborhood feature in the evenings and at night. The fact that this particular house was quiet effectively removed it from any sort of police radar. Toromillo had been looking for a place like it and bought if for cash, on the spot, the day the owner put up the "For Sale" sign.

It had been almost comical. Toromillo knocked on the door. A nine-year old child answered, then went to fetch her mother's live-in boyfriend.

"How much do you want for the house?" Toromillo asked.

The boyfriend quoted the price, then turned as if to close the door.

Toromillo said, "I'll throw in $15,000 more for everything in it if you get out by this afternoon."

The man turned back, open mouthed, looking at him.

Toromillo opened his brief case and pulled out four envelopes. The home owner could see they were full of hundred dollar bills.

The boyfriend turned and shouted to the young girl's mother, "Start packing your clothes, woman! We're getting out of this dump today!"

Toromillo's team came together, smuggled in from the *FARC* cadre over the southern border. For all the uproar over immigration among the gringos, getting into the country was simply a matter of knowing where and when to walk across. It didn't take many tugs on the strings of Toromillo's Venezuelan intelligence connections to get his elite group in.

He chuckled at Virrey's worries. "What will you tell them?" Virrey wondered.

"I won't tell them anything except the mission. These guys wouldn't want to know anyway," Toromillo said.

The moment Toromillo realized he was reassuring Virrey, he stopped. Let the bastard simmer, he thought. He's only putting up the money. We're the ones risking our asses.

The group spent the Spring and Summer training. They each made a point of flying in and out of Dallas Love Field, the in-town airport served by Southwest Airlines, as many times as it took to get comfortable. Through an associate in the airline, they kept tabs on what was flying out and where.

In late Summer, they bought a warehouse in an abandoned industrial park near Stephenville, Texas, a hundred miles away. Toromillo marked the outlines of the airport entry on the floor in chalk. The group practiced their attack until it was automatic.

Toromillo explained the plan to his team: "You can't hijack an American plane from inside anymore. Too much scrutiny. But in a smaller airport, you could storm a plane from outside if you have the right training and weaponry."

"What about when we get to Colombia?" one of them asked. "The whole fucking place is crawling with security. Airports especially."

"You can't storm your way out down there," Toromillo agreed. "But you can bribe your way out."

The men nodded.

"Makes sense to me," one of them said. "This will make the gringos pay attention."

"At the very least," Toromillo agreed.

Evans nervously crossed the street in front of the consulate and got into the back of the security officer's car. "I'll leave you just off the plaza," the guard said.

"Hell, I don't even know what this guy looks like," Evans complained.

"Somehow, I think he'll know who you are," the guard replied.

The car buzzed out into the swirling traffic. Evans still found himself holding on tight whenever he was in motion here. At an intersection, three cars tried to squeeze into one lane all at once. All three, including the consulate driver, leaned on their horns. Miraculously two of the cars made it and the third, the one Evans was in, fell back and took the next spot.

"Why do they drive like lunatics?" Evans groused.

"Why do we drive like pussies?" the guard answered.

He glanced in the rearview mirror to see Evans' reproachful look. "Oh, sorry sir," he hastily added.

The modern, tan granite plaza in front of the convention center was a block away from the waterfront, jammed at this hour with tourists and vendors. Since the lane closest to the sidewalk was torn up for construction, the consulate driver stopped Colombian style—in the middle of the street. Evans got out.

"I hope you know I hate this cloak and dagger shit," he snapped at the driver as he got out.

The driver said nothing. God, all that guy does is complain, he thought to himself.

Evans tiptoed through the asphalt onto the sidewalk. For all the destruction in the street, there was no sign of a construction crew. He walked slowly into the plaza, not knowing exactly what to do, feeling completely out of place. Under his shirt, he could feel the beads of sweat form again.

A quarter of the way across, there was still no one. Oh, there were plenty of people, but no one seemed to know him. Halfway across a vendor tried to sell him beads. "No, *gracias*," he said, while thinking Why is it always the goddamn beads?

Three quarters of the way across, he suddenly felt a hand on his arm from behind. Evans nearly jumped out of his skin. Sure he was being kidnaped, he turned suddenly and saw…his driver. "Señor Virrey is waiting for you over there. He was afraid you were lost."

"You know this guy," Evans asked.

The guard shook his head yes and said nothing. Evans was, again, amazed. The guard pointed out a well-dressed man in a fine suit, waving from under a tree. Evans walked over.

"Mr. Evans," Virrey said, "it was good of you to come. I apologize for the short notice."

Looking down at his watch, Virrey added, "You're only a little bit late."

"Not, not a problem," Evans stuttered. "What's this about a...."

Virrey cut him off with a strong hand motion. "Not here, Señor. Follow me."

He took Evans by the arm and led him across the plaza to where a Cadillac limousine, completely out of place on a Cartagena street, was waiting. The driver stepped around and opened the door. Evans hesitated.

"It's all right, Mr. Evans," Virrey said with a smile. "I promise not to kidnap you."

Evans didn't know whether Virrey was being comforting or condescending. He got in the car anyway. Virrey got in beside him. A heavy glass window shut the back compartment off from the driver's seat. "We can talk freely here," Virrey said, tapping on the glass.

The driver started the car and headed off into the honking traffic. "You...you said something about a murder in Dallas," Evans said.

"Yes, yes, very bad stuff unfortunately. I have some information that might be of interest to your government."

"What sort of information," Evans asked.

"We believe it was the work of a Venezuelan intelligence agent named Toromillo," Virrey answered, his eyes narrowing.

He handed over a large envelope and Evans opened it. Inside were pictures of the Venezuelan President meeting with Castro and Kim Jong-Il. Evans at least recognized them.

"Wh…, why are you handing me these?" he asked.

"This man here," Virrey said, pointing to a tall man with a bushy mustache wearing sunglasses in each picture, "this man is Toromillo. Very well placed in the Venezuelan service, wouldn't you say?"

"He must be," Evans agreed. "You're saying this man killed somebody in Dallas? What on earth for?"

"Not just somebody," Virrey corrected.

The car was careening up a hill leading to the La Popa seminary at the very top of Cartagena. Evans unconsciously was holding on tight to the armrest.

Virrey continued, "It was a high official in the American office of PDV, a man we believe…"

"What's PDV?" Evans asked for the second time that morning.

Virrey was momentarily silent, trying to decide whether this gringo was as naive as he seemed. Then he answered. "PDV, Mr. Evans, is *Petroleos de Venezuela*, the state oil company. We believe the man he killed was stealing drilling technology from American energy firms."

"Why would he do that?" Evans asked.

Then, thinking better of it, he asked "Who, exactly, is this 'we' you keep referring to?"

"I am in contact with a group of Venezuelan exiles opposed to communist rule in their country," Virrey said, gesturing at the photo of the Venezuelan President. "They passed along this information."

"Why are you passing it onto me?" Adams asked.

Virrey was beginning to get frustrated. Surely the man cannot be as incompetent as he seems, he thought.

"We believe that a murder committed in the United States by a Venezuelan intelligence agent should be of some interest to your government," Virrey said, impatience creeping into his own voice.

"Yes," Evans agreed, "I suppose it would."

"Furthermore," Virrey added, "we fear Toromillo has further plans in the United States."

"Further plans?" Evans asked.

"Yes, Señor. We believe he has gathered a team for some purpose while there. More than that we do not know."

"And what do you want me to do with…with this," Evans asked, holding the envelope.

"*Dios mío*, sir! We want you to inform your government!"

At that point the limo crunched into the gravel parking area at La Popa, high above the city. It was filled with tourists and, as always, street vendors. Virrey's driver pulled to a stop, stepped out and opened Evans' door. Virrey resumed his cordial demeanor: "Here we let you out, Mr. Vice-Consul. Enjoy the view!"

Evans stepped out of the car, holding the envelope and pictures. Virrey's driver closed Evans' door behind. The driver got back in, and the car crunched away. As his car pulled away, Virrey said to himself, "If that guy is the best the Americans can send us, God help them!"

A moment later the consular driver opened his door and motioned for Evans to get in. The two of them drove silently down the winding street back to the city.

Chapter Seven

Love Field in Dallas was a bustling place, having escaped closure in the early 1970s. Southwest Airlines, then a raw startup, had used a wrinkle in the law establishing the larger Dallas-Fort Worth International Airport to launch commuter flights from Love between the major Texas cities of Dallas, Houston, and San Antonio. From that modest start, Southwest had grown into the great white shark of the airline industry, consuming its rivals wherever it went.

Southwest's success had transformed the airport. The city had built gleaming new parking garages and terminals with long, air-conditioned walkways. There was even a museum on the Lemmon Avenue side of the field, showcasing the types of planes that had flown out of Love since its beginning as an Army Air Field in World War I.

There were two approaches to the concourse from which Southwest flew. One went through the cavernous main entry, past a bronze statue of an armed Texas Ranger. The Dallas Police kiosk was there, always manned. The Transportation Safety Administration ran Southwest's main passenger security point there as well, the line usually snaking well out onto the antique world map carved into the floor.

The secondary entry was up a flight of stairs, around the corner from the baggage claim. Families and friends awaited incoming passengers in the long hall there. This passageway was manned by two TSA guards, with one security checkpoint where the hall joined the concourse. The air conditioning often was not enough in this older part of the terminal. A huge fan kept the air moving around the checkpoint. There was always a Dallas police officer seated beside it, watching over the pedestrian traffic in and out of the restricted area.

Toromillo smiled to himself the very first time he saw the setup. This would be easy, he thought. Making matters easier was the fact that Southwest had recently been given permission to fly cross-country routes from Love Field as well. For years, flights had been restricted to Texas and the surrounding States, for fear of undermining the larger DFW Airport thirty miles away. After two decades of controversy, Southwest's success enabled them to bulldoze the so-called Wright Amendment and fly the longer flights.

Jabreel Daniels heard the alarm clock go off in his apartment south of I-30 on Jim Miller Road, in east Dallas. He stretched in bed, thought about going back to sleep, but got up anyway.

"Gotta keep food on the table," he mumbled to himself.

His wife was still asleep. So were the kids. He tiptoed into the kitchen in his bare feet, poured water into a coffee cup, then zapped it in the microwave. Two minutes later he was stretched out in his ratty old recliner, sipping the coffee and watching TV.

He woke with a start about half an hour later when his wife walked in.

"Jabreel, aren't you working today?" she asked.

"Oh shit!" he said, jumping to his feet and spilling the rest of the coffee on himself as he did so.

Five minutes later he had on his white Transportation Safety Authority shirt, black pants, and black shoes, rushing out of the apartment and down the stairs to the car. He drove an old Plymouth Neon, much to his children's embarrassment. At least it ran, he thought. He fired it up, pulled up to the electric gate, and punched in his code to open it. Sometimes it worked on the first try and sometimes it didn't. This morning it worked like a charm.

Jabreel, like so many others, landed the TSA job after 9/11, as America mobilized its defenses against terrorism. He'd been a security guard before, making $7.50 an hour to sit in the lobby of a downtown skyscraper all night. The TSA gig was a lot better. The pay was a little higher, but the job came with government benefits and a paid vacation. Each time he cashed his paycheck, he couldn't help remembering how many of the kids he'd grown up with on Jim Miller Road who were either dead or in prison.

Jabreel joked with his family a few months into the job that the security was so tight nobody could get anything through. He also said, "Of course, they could always come up, shoot my ass, and walk through if they wanted."

"Ain't nobody gonna shoot your ass at the airport," his brother said. "The Dallas cops are always there."

"Yeah," Jabreel answered, "reading their damn magazines. They'd probably shoot me by mistake."

"Mistake, hell!" his brother said. "Somebody comes up with a gun, cops are always gonna shoot you first! Don't matter who else they shoot!"

They all laughed.

Jabreel cruised up Jim Miller toward the freeway. The road was lined with Spanish-language businesses. There seemed to be more of them every day. When he was kid there hadn't been any. Dallas had been strictly a black and white affair.

"Damn illegals," he said to himself. "It's like an invasion."

He thought about stopping for more coffee, looked at his watch, and decided not to. As he topped the bridge on Miller over the freeway, his heart sank to see jammed traffic stretching out toward downtown.

"Hell," he whispered. "I hope they don't fire my ass."

He wove his way through the traffic, circled north of downtown on Woodall Rogers, and reached the employee parking lot at Love Field with five minutes to spare. Jabreel sprinted through the airport. He was gasping for breath when he showed his credentials and passed through the employee checkpoint.

"Morning, Jabreel," the guard on duty said. "Got your badge with you?"

"Same badge as yesterday," Jabreel laughed.

It seemed absurd to have to flash the same ID every single day to the same people, but those were the rules. He grabbed his second cup of coffee from the employee break room, then walked to his post. His job was to herd the passengers who came up the wrong way, as he considered it, through the secondary baggage check.

This morning, a fully-fueled Southwest 737-700 sat at Gate One, waiting to take off to Portland Airport in Oregon. The passengers were boarding in Southwest's customary blocks of thirty, with the flight crew reminding all aboard, "This will be a full flight."

As the Southwest plane went through its boarding process, a gray Chevy Suburban with blackened windows pulled to a stop outside the baggage claim in a parking area restricted to taxis and buses. The Dallas police officer on duty walked over amiably to tell the driver to move on.

As he approached, the four doors on both sides of the car plus the rear hatch swung open at once. Eight heavily armed men in black flack vests and ski masks jumped out at once. One of them pointed his silenced pistol at the officer's head and fired.

The officer sprawled to the ground, a pool of blood forming around his shattered skull. The gunshot made no noise. The bystanders were slow to react. By the time two other Dallas cops took the scene in and began fiddling for their guns, a fusillade of silenced rounds cut them down as well. The eight attackers sprinted into the building.

As Toromillo expected, there was nothing to stop them inside. They thundered up the stairs, hurtling past the startled people waiting for their deplaning loved ones. Two quick shots took out the heavyset women guarding the post midway down the hall.

The assailants reached the far end of the hall before any sort of alarm sounded. Jabreel Daniel saw them coming and shouted, "Wait! You have to go through the line!"

They shot him down before he could say anything else. The sole Dallas officer, scrambling for his weapon, was shot dead too. The attackers bounded passed the security point, setting off alarm bells all over the building. At that exact moment, the car bomb inside the gray SUV detonated with a shattering blast in front of the terminal.

The men rushed the passenger gangway at Gate One, pushing stragglers out of their way and forcing their way onto the plane. They fanned out throughout it, guns drawn. The cockpit door was still open. Toromillo ordered the flight attendant and Captain to stand back from it and close the outside door. They did.

"Now," Toromillo said to the Captain, "fly the plane."

"I won't do it," he said. David Newman, the Captain, had retired from the Navy as a carrier pilot. His warrior instincts were unfortunate, however.

Toromillo grabbed the closest flight attendant and put the gun to her head. "Fly it," he said.

"I won't," Newman insisted.

Toromillo pulled the trigger. The specially made round exploded into the woman's skull, stopping without making an exit wound. She slumped to the floor. The passengers began screaming.

Toromillo grabbed the next flight attendant and put the gun to her head. "Fly the plane," he commanded.

This time the Captain complied.

Chapter Eight

Word of the car bombing and hijacking at Dallas Love Field shook the city to its core. Within minutes, fleets of fire engines, ambulances, and Dallas police were in route. They arrived on a scene from hell.

All the windows in the building were blown out. Bodies and parts of bodies were strewn throughout the parking and baggage check areas. Anything in the vicinity that could burn was on fire. As the first detachments arrived, a rogue 737 thundered into the air.

Onboard, Toromillo took the flight plan from his pocket and gave it to the First Officer, bracing to stand up as the plane climbed sharply into the sky. Another hijacker kept his gun trained on the pilot from the First Officer's seat inside the cockpit. Reinforced doors would make no difference this time.

The First Officer, looking at the neatly typed flight plan, asked him, "Where the hell is Mitú, Colombia?"

"It's a lovely place," Toromillo said sarcastically. "You'll feel right at home."

By the time the plane reached cruising altitude, word of the terrorist attack was reaching the highest levels of the American government. Most people in and out of government assumed the attackers were *Al Qaeda*. In the State Department's Office of Latin American Consular Affairs, though, a clerk fished through her desk top for a manila envelope full of photos containing a memo from a Vice-Consul named Evans in Colombia. It had arrived a few days before.

She hadn't paid particular attention to it beyond stamping it with the day and time, skimming it briefly, and putting it in her file. Now, with news of the attack flying through the office, she remembered it clearly and took it to her supervisor.

"I think you should see this," she said. "It came in three days ago."

An hour later the Secretary of State laid the envelope on the President's desk in the Oval Office. The President's face reddened with anger as she briefed him on its contents.

"This son of a bitch, this…what's his name?" the President said.

"Toromillo, sir," the Secretary replied.

"This son of a bitch Toromillo's been in the country, we've had this information, and we did nothing about it?" he raged.

"Sir," one of the generals in the room said, "we're watching a lot of stuff these days. This information only came in three days ago."

"Goddamn it!" the President exploded.

He fancied himself as someone who did not regularly use profanity. He'd now used it three times in two minutes. His aides winced.

"Who sent this to us?" the President asked, regaining a bit of composure.

"A consular officer from Cartagena, Colombia. A man named, uh, Evans," the Secretary said, pausing to read the man's name among the notes. "He's an old Colombia hand," she said, reading his bio. "Really knows the country well. Obviously has good contacts."

"Fly him up here now! I want his take on this!" the President ordered.

The Secretary of State said, "I'll get right on it."

She dispatched one of her staff members to make arrangements.

"Now, his source says the Venezuelans and the *FARC* are behind this, not *Al Qaeda*?" the President queried.

"That's what he says, sir," the Secretary answered.

The President's face reddened again. "Well I'll be DAMNED if I'll let that bastard Perez or some Colombian drug dealer attack this country without consequences!"

"Sir," the Attorney General said, "we have to look at this source carefully. It could be disinformation."

"Carefully, hell!" the President raged. "Look here!" he said, fumbling through the photos in a blind fury "It's got pictures of the bastard with *Presidente* Perez in North Korea with Kim goddamn Jong-Il," he shouted.

"True, sir," he said, "but we still have to check out the source."

"Check it out, then," he snapped.

Turning to the Chairman of the Joint Chiefs, he said, "What do we have in the region?"

"Well, sir," the General said, "it's our back yard. If Venezuela and the *FARC* are behind it, we could hit them with practically everything we have by this time tomorrow."

"Good," the President said. "I want my options ASAP."

"Yes sir," the General said. He immediately sent his chief of staff out with his aides to begin the planning.

"Sir," the Secretary of State said, "we can't do anything until we know for sure."

The President replied, "You know as well as I do that we can never know 'for sure!' We've got to get ready! The American people will demand it!"

Aboard the plane, the passengers had returned to a semblance of calm. Toromillo took the mike and addressed them. "Please forgive us for the unplanned schedule change. I assure you that no one else will be hurt if everyone cooperates."

"Are you going to fly us into a building?" one the passengers screamed.

"No, no, no," Toromillo said, as soothingly as he could. "We're not Arabs. This isn't a suicide mission, unless you make it one."

"Who are you?" another passenger shouted.

"We represent the *Fuerzas Armadas Revolucionarias de Colombia*," he answered. "We intend to draw attention to the struggle of the poorest of the poor in Colombia."

As Toromillo expected, a dozen passengers were now whispering the attackers' identity through cell phones to loved ones on the ground.

Chapter Nine

News reports soon became a torrent as major global media converged on Dallas. Not since the Kennedy assassination had the city garnered this level of attention. CNN headlined its "Breaking News" coverage "Atrocity and Terror in Dallas." Fox, MSNBC, the major networks, and the worldwide press tuned in equally.

The initial suspicion fell on Islamist terrorism, as always. Panicked bystanders reported only seeing masked gunmen storming the airport, then the shattering explosion. In Washington, the US government was trying mightily to keep a lid on its suspicions, even as the Southwest plane flew south toward the Gulf of Mexico.

Some secrets are hard to keep. Within thirty minutes of the incident's beginning, CNN, citing an "anonymous State Department source," announced that official suspicion was falling on a suspected agent of the Venezuelan intelligence services. Someone inside State had leaked Evans' memo and the Toromillo photos.

Within minutes of that, the media began broadcasting stories of what family members on the ground were hearing on their cellular conversations with loved ones in the air. Word of the *FARC* connection became global knowledge. Predictably, the major networks began ginning together informational pieces on both the situation in Venezuela and the history of the Colombian insurgency.

It soon became clear on the ground that this was no repeat of 9/11. Under Toromillo's orders, the plane steered well clear of major metropolitan areas and their skyscrapers. He intended to give the American F-16s tailing it no reason to shoot it down.

As America's attentions focused on the airborne drama, the public reaction to the alleged Venezuelan and Colombian connections built quickly. People who hardly knew the names of either country an hour before were being quoted on the air calling for immediate air strikes. The President's Press Secretary addressed the media from a jammed White House Press Room, reminding the nation and world that the identity of the terrorists was as yet unknown.

"America will respond forcefully when things become clearer," he assured the nation.

Ivan Marez, from the Venezuelan Embassy in Bogotá, first heard the news of the terrorist attack as he was finishing a session in *La Dollhouse*, a notorious brothel in Bogotá's *Zona de Tolerancia* (Tolerance Zone). The initial reports made no mention of Venezuela or of Toromillo. Marez muttered an obscenity under his breath about Americans, paid for his session, and went out to meet his driver in the street.

During the ride back to the Embassy, his cell phone rang. He noticed with pleasure Ana Restrepo's number on his caller ID. "Maybe I'll have dessert with my dinner," he said to the driver before he answered.

Restrepo didn't sound dessert-like when he said hello. "Have you heard the news from Dallas?" she asked.

"Yes," he said. "Off the record, this serves the Americans right."

There was shocked silence on the other end of the line. Marez thought perhaps the phone had gone dead. "Ana," he said, "are you there?"

"Did you just say 'it serves the Americans right'?" she asked, incredulously.

"Off the record of course, my dear," he soothed.

Ana asked, "Have you heard most recent report?"

She couldn't hide the consternation in her voice.

"No," he answered, "I'm going back to the Embassy from a…a meeting. What are they saying?"

"CNN is quoting a State Department source saying the hijackers are connected to your country's intelligence service!"

Marez yelled so loudly his driver nearly ran into the back of a bus.

Aboard the plane, the hijackers separated the women and children from the men, putting the former at the back of the plane. As they did so, they began checking the identification papers of their captives. Since the hijacked flight was domestic, there were no passports. Drivers' licenses, State IDs, and credit cards were enough. As they were checking through them, they ran across one unexpected treasure: a Congressional ID bearing the name James Cook, R-TX.

Cook represented the arch-conservative southwestern suburbs of Houston. He had a national reputation as one of the most bitterly partisan right-wingers in the President's party. The hijacker who discovered the ID gleefully showed it to Toromillo.

"The man is pure gold," Toromillo said smiling. "Bring him to me."

Two of the hijackers brought him forward, pistols pressed against the back of his head. "So you are the famous Mr. Cook," Toromillo said.

"What are your plans for this plane?" the Congressman demanded.

"We're not the minority party up here, Congressman," Toromillo said. "Don't address us as if we were."

Toromillo hauled Cook into the cockpit and thrust the radio communicator into his hand. "Now, Congressman, you will repeat exactly what I tell you."

Cook hesitated. Toromillo smacked him upside the head with the barrel of his pistol. The Congressman staggered, then stood erect, one eye closing in pain.

"Identify yourself to them," Toromillo ordered.

Cook spoke into the mike. "This is US Representative James Cook."

The ground controllers answered immediately. "We read you, Congressman Cook. What is your situation?"

"Tell them everyone is fine," Toromillo said. Looking down at the dead flight attendant he corrected himself. "Almost everyone."

"Almost everyone is fine," Cook answered.

"Who is in control of the plane?" the controller answered.

"Tell him the plane is in the custody of the *Fuerzas Armadas Revolucionarias de Colombia*," Toromillo ordered.

"The plane is in the custody of the '*Forzas Armadas Revolutionistas de Colombia*,'" Cook said, murdering the Spanish name of the Colombian guerrillas.

Those listening on the ground understood exactly who he meant.

"Tell them," Toromillo said with a slight smile, "we will release passengers and crew unharmed if we are not interfered with."

Cook, seeing the cynical smile, sputtered, "You bastard!"

Toromillo raised his finger in a mocking rebuke. The Congressman did as he was told.

"That's a good boy," Toromillo said, as if he were talking to a dog.

Colombian army trucks are commonplace in Mitú, especially in the years since the military had begun its offensive against the *FARC* in the surrounding jungles. Five more had been driven into the town and parked near the National Police checkpoint in the previous two weeks, unnoticed.

Communication between the National Police and the army was intermittent, even during wartime. The National Police had been infiltrated many times by the guerrillas, making them suspect in the army's eyes. A recent expose in the Colombian magazine *Pensamiento* had detailed police infiltrators' roles in kidnaping and selling "high value individuals" to the *FARC*. This suspicion, coupled with the ordinary fog of war, allowed five men dressed as soldiers to get into the trucks and drive them to the long ribbon of concrete masquerading as Mitú's airport in the jungle. Again, nobody thought anything was out of place.

In the air, Southwest Captain David Newman was trying frantically to think of a way to rescue the plane as it flew over the Gulf toward Colombia. Every scenario he thought of seemed impossible. The disaster behind them in Dallas and the dead body of his chief flight attendant told him all he needed to know about the determination of the attackers.

He had to try something, though, he thought. "Excuse me, sir," he said to Toromillo. "This plane isn't carrying enough fuel to fly to Colombia."

Toromillo was ready with an answer. "Of course it is, Captain. We know exactly how far this plane can fly. Trust me," he said, smiling his cynical smile. "We researched this project very carefully."

The hijacker seated in the cockpit laughed at Toromillo's joke.

"Well," Newman said, frantic to find some way out, "this is a big plane. It can't land on a dirt strip in the jungle."

Toromillo laughed again. "I assure you, Captain, thanks to your American generosity the airstrip in Mitú can handle a plane like this. I've checked it out personally."

In the main cabin, the passengers' anxiety grew with each passing minute. The men onboard, herded to the front, sat there under the watchful eyes of the gunmen. In the rear, women and children sat in cold terror, many of them crying. Some had vomited into the airsickness bags.

A woman asked for permission to use the restroom. One of the hijacker's snapped back, "Nobody gets out of their seat. Pee in your pants if you have to."

Toromillo agreed. "Shoot anyone who gets out of a seat," he instructed the hijackers over the loudspeaker. "There won't be any Todd Beamers on this flight."

Chapter Ten

On the ground, the American government and military could only watch helplessly as the plane flew south. As yet, they had no idea of its destination, though it was obviously headed for South America. Media outlets soon broadcast Congressman Cook's choked voice identifying the *'Forzas Armadas Revolutionistas de Colombia'* to the world.

That bit of news came as a huge shock to the *FARC* leadership. Venezuelan President Perez and his cabinet reacted with equal shock reporters announced Jorge Toromillo's name and his connection to the Venezuelan intelligence services began filling the airwaves. CNN was the first to show a photo of a man they identified Toromillo to the global audience. In the photo, Toromillo was standing beside President Perez and Kim Jong-il.

Perez felt his knees begin to tremble. CNN followed Toromillo's photo with a clip of Perez himself insulting of the American Secretary of State. He watched himself on television saying, "Don't mess with me, Madam—I bite."

"Where is Toromillo?" he demanded.

"In the United States," the intelligence chief replied.

Perez and Toromillo had known each other for decades. They served together in the elite Venezuelan special forces. Toromillo had been at Perez's side when the latter had been ousted from the Venezuelan military for political activities. It nearly cost both men their lives. Mariano Perez simply couldn't wrap his mind around the idea that Toromillo had betrayed him.

"What…why…" Perez couldn't even form the words. He groped for them a moment or two and said, "The CIA is setting us up! Get the American Secretary of State on the phone now!"

The Foreign Minister ran out of the room to see to the call. A few tense minutes later he reappeared. "She is not available," he said. "Her spokesman would only say they are evaluating the situation."

On the TV screen, CNN came back on after a *Levitra* commercial. "Although the evidence at this point is still circumstantial, much of what we have discovered during the three hours of this standoff points straight at the government of Venezuelan President Perez…"

"Goddamn it! Tell the Americans I had nothing to do with this!" Perez shouted.

"I did, sir," the Foreign Minister replied.

"What did they say?" he demanded.

"Sir, they would only say they are 'evaluating the situation.'"

"Good God," Perez whispered. "We have to get those passengers back, wherever that goddamn plane lands! If the Americans believe we did this…"

He couldn't bring himself to finish the sentence.

A thousand miles away in Vaupés, the *FARC* high command was reaching the same conclusion.

In Cartagena, an armored limousine escorted by heavily-armed Colombian soldiers pulled to a stop in front of the American consulate. The security guard opened the door and the soldiers escorted Don

Evans to the car. It was the second time in a week he had ridden in the back of a limousine.

This time it sped him with his armed escort through the streets of the city to the door of a chartered jet, waiting at the airport to fly him to Washington. This time there were no problems with the city's traffic. When Evans was aboard, the jet streaked into the air from Cartagena. About the same time, the Southwest plane crossed into Colombian airspace from the Caribbean.

Chapter Eleven

Five hours after its grisly beginning, the Southwest flight was over Colombia. Toromillo had been careful not to allow anyone but the Captain and First Officer to know the name of the destination, Mitú. Now, forty-five minutes away, it was time to let the rest of the world in on the secret.

He called Congressman Cook to the cabin and thrust the radio into his hands. "Tell them we're going to Mitú. Tell them to get the Colombian army out of the way or everyone dies!"

"Wh…Where?" Cook stammered.

He'd never heard of the place.

"We're going to Mitú," Toromillo repeated slowly. "To *Meee-tooo*. Tell them to get the army out of the way or we'll blow the plane up when we land."

Cook held the mike to his mouth. "The man says we are going to a place called Mitú. He says to clear the Colombian army out of the way or he will blow up the plane and kill everyone."

The passengers close enough to hear this gasped. Word spread back through the cabin. The sound of sobs and crying filled the air again.

The voice of the ground controllers crackled in. "Roger, Congressman. Mitú. Clear the army. We'll pass the word onto the Colombians."

"Is it safe to land there?!" the Congressman blurted out over the air, tears forming in his eyes.

Toromillo hadn't given him permission to speak. He pressed the pistol against the Congressman's temple and pretended to pull the trigger. "Pow!" he shouted.

A black stain darkened the inside of the Congressman's pants. Cook had pissed himself.

Once the name Mitú was spoken, wheels began turning in Washington, Bogotá, and Caracas, as well as in the jungles of Vaupés. The American Ambassador to Colombia immediately called the State Department for instructions. Colombian President Arena radioed his army commanders on the ground to secure the airport. President Perez in Caracas ordered his intelligence agency to prepare a covert rescue mission into Colombia. The leaders of the *FARC* ordered the commander of their local front, Ernesto Botero, to also prepare a rescue mission.

Washington replied immediately to the Ambassador. He was instructed to ask the Colombian army to maintain a perimeter around the airport and detain the hijackers there as long as possible. The US offered American Marines. Arena politely declined. The Colombian army needed no help on its own soil, he said.

Sleepy little Mitú sprang to life in the late afternoon. Colombian army and police units were on the move everywhere. A column of five army trucks commanded by a man in a Colonel's uniform waited with the rest of the soldiers on the perimeter of the airport. Captain Miguel Escalante, called back from the jungle with his elite combat force, was racing in to lead a strike on the plane, should it be necessary.

Escalante stopped at the perimeter alongside the trucks. "The plane is definitely coming here?" he asked the Colonel.

"Yes, Captain," the Colonel replied. "We got the word from Bogotá."

"What are these trucks for?" Escalante asked.

"We're here to pick up the passengers when they are released," the other man answered.

It seemed perfectly reasonable.

The plane began its descent in the fading sunlight. Toromillo ordered the men seated in the first four rows to be ready to follow him as soon as the plane landed. The hijackers cocked their weapons conspicuously. More shrieks and sobbing filled the air.

Escalante and his soldiers readied their weapons too as they heard the plane approaching. Botero, leading a guerrilla contingent, had taken up a position in a carefully concealed observation post. He watched the plane come in through binoculars, taking time also to scan the Colombian soldiers gathered around the airport's perimeters. At one point he stared directly into the face of Miguel Escalante.

The lumbering 737 came in from the northwest, its landing gear in place, its tires squealing as it bumped to the ground on the concrete strip. The Captain reversed the thrusters and pulled as hard as he could on the controls, struggling to bring the plane to a stop. It finally rolled to a halt a good twenty meters from the end of the strip.

To Escalante's amazement, the Colonel and his trucks immediately moved out in a convoy toward the front of the plane, where the hatch was opening.

"Hey, wait!" Escalante shouted.

The Colonel pointed to his radio and shouted back, "They told us to go in! Stay back!"

Escalante wavered a moment, but stayed put. He'd heard no instructions on his radio.

On the plane, Toromillo ordered the surviving flight attendant to open the door. As soon as she did so, he dumped the body of the slain attendant onto the tarmac.

"Inflate the slide," he commanded.

The attendant pulled a lever and the emergency slide blew into position below them. Five trucks were approaching at high speed across the tarmac. Toromillo and one of the hijackers slid down first, then took positions with guns ready at the bottom. Another kept his weapon trained on Captain Newman and the First Officer.

As the trucks pulled to a stop beside the plane, the rest of the hijackers hustled twenty male passengers, including Congressman Cook and Captain Newman, to the hatch and down the slide. The assailants immediately followed.

With clockwork precision, the hijackers herded the men into groups of four in the backs of the trucks. Escalante, watching from several hundred meters away, suddenly realized what was going on and ordered his men forward. Unfortunately, they were on foot. They couldn't risk opening fire at that distance, not knowing who or what they might hit.

At the airport fence just meters from the plane, a National Police detachment bribed by the hijackers detonated a series of small explosives, knocking that portion of the fence flat. The trucks, hostages secured, roared through the opening before other army units in the area knew what was going on. In an instant, the convoy disappeared down a road leading into the jungle.

Five hundred meters further, the trucks roared to a halt. The hijackers again herded the hostages out with brutal efficiency. They stumbled down an embankment in the darkening jungle. Five small, motorized launches were waiting. In a matter of seconds, all the hostages were aboard. The boats roared off into the jungle without a shot being fired.

By the time Escalante and his men had sprinted the length of the runway and reached the parked trucks, there was no sign of hijackers or hostages. They had disappeared into the jungle night.

Escalante caught his breath, then commanded half of his troops to secure the trucks. He led the other half on a sprint back to the airfield.

While he was gone, the remaining flight attendants had popped open the hatches on both sides of the plane. The soldiers at the airport had driven the portable stairways halfway to the plane, then stopped. Escalante, drenched in sweat, swore at the top of his lungs to the drivers of the stalled stairways.

"Get those things to the plane!" he ordered.

Both Escalante and the nearest driver yelled at the same time, "It might be booby-trapped!"

To Escalante that meant 'Rescue as many as we can before it blows!' To the others it meant 'Stay out of range!'

Disgusted by their cowardice, Escalante ran to the closest vehicle and threw its driver out of the seat. He jumped in and slammed his foot on the accelerator. The awkward vehicle lurched forward toward the plane.

The flight attendants were helping women and children down the two inflated slides as fast as they could. Those amidships stood back as Escalante slammed the stairway into the hatch door. He pulled up hard on the locking brake, flung himself out onto the tarmac, and leapt up the stairs into the plane. Two other soldiers were close behind.

The passengers still in the plane screamed when they saw him, thinking he was another terrorist. He didn't have either the English skills or the time to explain otherwise. As quickly as he could, he began pushing the passengers toward the other soldiers, who had positioned themselves at the top and bottom of the stairway. They frantically maneuvered the people to the stairs.

It took less than two minutes to get the able-bodied passengers off the plane. "*Corre! Corre!* (Run! Run!), the soldiers shouted at them in Spanish when they hit the ground, making running motions with their arms. The Americans needed little encouragement.

Finally, only two young children and two elderly women remained. "*Ven, muchachos!* (Come on, boys!)" Escalante shouted to his troops.

He scooped up the two children, one under each arm, and bounded down the stairs with them. The next soldier lifted an elderly American woman on his back and followed. Escalante handed the children to a waiting soldier on the ground and sprinted back up the stairs. One elderly woman remained, frantically trying to stuff the contents of her purse back inside from where they had spilled.

As he reached her, Escalante heard the ringing of a cell phone from one of the forward hatches. He threw the old woman to the floor and hurled his body over her as the ringing phone triggered the detonator in the bomb. Instead of the shattering explosion he expected, Escalante heard only a loud pop. The detonator seemed to have misfired.

He looked up and saw flames beginning to leap out of the sealed compartment. Grabbing the poor woman by her arms he flung her over his shoulder and sprinted down the stairs. They had just reached the tarmac when the delayed fuse on the bomb exploded.

There was no word from the assailants who had escaped into the darkness. The Colombian jungle is an immense, impenetrable natural refuge and the men who had fled into it obviously knew it well. Only a few salient facts were clear as the sun rose. Terrorists had succeeded in a brazen attack on an American airport. A hijacked plane had been flown into a remote, embattled region in the Colombian jungle. The attackers, aided by corrupt police and incompetent soldiers, had escaped. The Southwest plane sat destroyed on the runway.

Later in the day other facts became clear. Clandestine cell phone photos taken by passengers revealed that the lead hijacker was, in fact, Jorge Toromillo. Cockpit voice transcripts confirmed that Toromillo and his gang had acted in the name of the *FARC*. The American FBI confirmed that it had tracked Toromillo for some time in the United States on suspicion of spying for Venezuela, before losing track of him. And at the top and bottom of each hour, all the major news outlets rebroadcast both the photos of Toromillo with Venezuelan President Perez, as well as Perez's recent denunciation of the American Secretary of State.

By early afternoon, the mayor of Caracas had to send riot police out into the streets to put a lid on the ugly, anti-Perez demonstrations that were breaking out like brush fires. At the same time, crowds of angry American citizens were demonstrating in front of the Venezuelan Embassy in Washington. Perez denied through his spokesmen any knowledge of or participation in the hijacking and expressed sympathies for the families of the victims. The State Department in Washington responded to the Venezuelan Foreign Minister's insistent calls by saying only that it was reviewing the situation.

When he woke up the following morning at a military hospital in Bogotá, Miguel Escalante found out he had become an international hero. A video crew at the airport captured his frantic dash to the portable stairway and his heroic rescue of the remaining passengers. Miraculously, even the old woman he last carried down the stairwell had survived the blast, which in the end left the plane a shattered, burned out hulk.

Colombia needed a hero at that moment. The media were broadcasting around the world the treachery of its National Police, who had cooperated with the terrorists in their escape. The whole world also saw the seeming incompetence of its army, which had been duped into allowing terrorists to drive escape trucks up to the plane itself.

Chapter Twelve

Don Evans was ushered into the Oval Office first thing in the morning, carrying a copy of the report he had sent to Washington four days earlier. The President and his top advisors greeted him as a hero.

"Mr. Evans," the President said, "I realize you probably risked your life to get this information. I am so very sorry we didn't act in time."

Evans didn't quite know what to say, so he said, "Thank you, sir."

"Fill us in on this fellow who gave you the information," the President asked.

When Evans gave him an uncertain look, the Secretary of State motioned to the report he had in his hand. "Oh this," Evans said. "Yes, well…the man's name was Hernan Virrey."

"How do we know he wasn't planting the story?" the Attorney General asked.

The President said, "I'd say we know because what the man warned us about happened. Why would someone warn us just to plant a story?"

He sat there quietly a moment, pondering the stakes. Then he turned to Don Evans and said, "What do you think?"

Evans had never been asked his opinion by the President of the United States before. All he could say was, "I agree with you, sir. Why would he give us advance warning if he was only planting a story?"

The President was palpably relieved. "I'm glad we've got men like you in our Foreign Service," he said, standing up to clap Evans on the back. "By God, next time we'll have to listen closer."

He turned and addressed Evans again. "I want you to do something for me personally, Mr. Evans. Will you?"

"Yes sir," Evans replied, taken aback that the President of the United States would ask him a personal favor. "Of course."

"I want you to personally go to Colombia and see to bringing those poor souls back home. God knows they've been through enough hell already. I want to see 'em in your capable hands on the way back. That'll help all of us sleep better."

Everyone in the room nodded in agreement. Evans could only reply, "Of course, sir. I'll handle it myself."

Inside, though, Evans was shaking his head and thinking do I have to go back to that godforsaken place again?

The day after the attack, Ana Restrepo sifted through the accounts of terrorized eyewitnesses in Mitú, worried sick about Miguel Escalante. She had flown to an airstrip near the jungle city as soon as Mitú been mentioned, riding by jeep into the town itself. The main airport, needless to say, was closed.

Her cell phone rang two different times that morning. Neither call was from Miguel.

The first call was from Ivan Marez at the Venezuelan Embassy in Bogotá.

"Ana," he pleaded, "you have to help us! Caracas is panicking. You have to help us get the word to the Americans that we had nothing to do with this!"

Restrepo replied coldly, "That didn't seem to be your story when this all started."

Her reply made him even more frantic. "Ana, I had no idea! I never intended it to sound like our government condoned attacking innocent civilians!"

"Let me check my notes," she said. "Ah, yes. Here they are. You said, and I quote, 'It serves the Americans right.'"

"Ana," he cried. "That was off the record!"

"Maybe I need to set the record straight," she said.

She felt a cool satisfaction making this vile man squirm.

"But Ana," he continued, "they might attack our country!"

"Didn't you say you had advised your President to tell the American Secretary of State—again, I quote—'Do not mess with me, Madam. I bite'?"

"Oh *Dios*, Ana," Marez said, all but weeping into the phone. "Those were just words! Words!"

"Is this the moment when President Perez bites the Secretary of State, Ivan? Or do you think she'll do the biting?"

With that, she hung up the phone.

The second call came from a number she didn't recognize. She heard an unfamiliar voice, sounding like it was coming from the bottom of a well. Phone service from rural Colombia often sounded like that, when it was available at all. "Ms. Restrepo, from the magazine *Pensamiento?*" the voice queried.

"Yes, this is Ana Restrepo from *Semana*," she answered. "Who is speaking?"

"My name is Ernesto Botero" the voice said. "It is very important that I meet with you as soon as possible. I personally guarantee your safety."

Chapter Thirteen

By late afternoon, a US Air Force C-130, escorted by American F-16 fighters, was touching down in Mitú, carrying a contingent of US Marines, a medical team, and a cohort from the State Department led by Don Evans. This time the Colombians had no choice but to accept the American "offer" of troops. The plane taxied to a position midway between the shattered airliner and the ramshackle terminal.

Before the rear hatch opened, Evans reminded all aboard, "This is Colombia. Don't trust anyone!"

As soon as the C-130's rear deck swung down to the tarmac, the Marines stormed off with their weapons locked and loaded to form a defensive perimeter. They pointed their weapons directly at the Colombian soldiers gathered at various points around the airfield. The F-16s screamed in low for added effect. The Colombians stepped back, visibly shaken by the foreign soldiers threatening them on their own soil.

Evans led the State Department contingent and the medical team off the plane and into the terminal to begin the process of bringing the shocked survivors home. The major media outlets covered his dramatic appearance, broadcasting to the world a face they assumed was lined with worry. Every step he took was accompanied by a phalanx of battle-ready Marines.

As Evans was making his triumphal entry into Mitú, Air Force One was descending into shattered Love Field in Dallas. The President and his key advisors were already discussing the political fallout from the attack.

"You know," the Press Secretary said, "the Democrats'll roast us alive for having this information three days without acting on it."

The Attorney General said, "They know how big the government is, Stan. Three days warning is nothing with as much information as we have coming in every day. They wouldn't use a tragedy like this for political purposes."

"The hell they wouldn't!," the Press Secretary said. "We certainly would. With all due respect, State's got to get off its ass and forward things like this up the chain of command faster."

The Secretary of State bristled. "'Things like this'?" she said indignantly. "Blown up airports and hijacked planes? I'm sorry, but 'Things like this' don't come up the chain of command everyday!"

"Tell that to the vultures in the press when we land," he snapped back.

"All right, all right, that's enough," the President cut in. "What we have to do now is appear decisive. How sure is the link between Toromillo and the Venezuelans?"

"One hundred percent, sir," the Attorney General answered, somewhat reluctantly. "We've got photographic evidence of him with Perez in North Korea. Highly-important trip for them, highest possible level of security. No way Toromillo's on that play unless he's a major, major player inside the Venezuelan government."

"And how sure are we Toromillo was on our plane," the President asked, making sure.

"Photographic, sir. At least two of the passengers got him on their cell cameras in flight. He was there," the Attorney General answered.

"Do we want to consider the chance he's a double agent?" the Attorney General asked again.

The President ignored the question. No one else offered an answer.

"Toromillo himself said he was with the goddamn Colombian rebels on the plane, didn't he?" the President said, breaking the silence.

The Secretary of State answered, "Yes, Mr. President. We've got it on tape."

"Well, it's open and shut then. This thing has Perez's fingerprints all over it, plus it proves Venezuela's working with the…what do you call them?"

He fumbled for the name.

"With the *FARC*," the Secretary of State answered.

"The question isn't who did it, then," the President answered. "It's what the hell are we going to do about it. I think the American people will forgive us three days if we go after the assholes behind this with both fists.

"General," he said to the Chairman of the Joint Chiefs, "are we ready to go?"

The Secretary of State interrupted. "Excuse me, sir. It seems like our hands our tied until we find out about the hostages."

"We don't negotiate with hostage-takers!" the President raged. "From this moment forward that includes goddamn *Presidente* Perez and the Venezuelan government!"

"Mr. President," the Attorney General said, "we need to be completely clear about the consequences of this. I know it looks like Perez and the *FARC* are behind this, but I've been in enough courtrooms to know that appearances can be deceiving. If we go to war and it turns out to have been a deception…"

He didn't finish the sentence. The others pondered what he said for a silent moment.

One of the generals broke in. "Maybe," he said. "But if we can use this to destroy the *FARC* and get rid of this bastard Perez, things will be better for us in Latin American in general…even if we were wrong."

"That's completely immoral!" the Attorney General shot back, cutting him off.

"That's life in the real world!" the Press Secretary said.

The President paused for a moment, the anguish visible on his face. Then he gave the order. "I don't see that we have any choice. We have to hit 'em and hit 'em hard enough that no one else will even think about doing this to us again. NEVER, EVER AGAIN!"

The Chairman of the Joint Chiefs saluted and left the room.

"God," the President added, "why is it always more war?"

The Amazon jungle is literally unforgiving territory. Those who visit it are required to have vaccinations against yellow fever. A host of other measures need to be taken to guard against lethal insects and snakes, as well as against the ever-present hordes of malarial mosquitos. The American hostages, dressed for a trip to Portland, Oregon, were obviously unprepared.

Very early the morning after the hijacking, one of the younger hostages ran afoul of a huge scorpion with a red dot on its tail. Not realizing the danger, he didn't get out of the way fast enough to keep the thing from stinging him through his sock. The pain was intense and searing.

By late afternoon, the man could no longer walk. His ankle was grotesquely swollen, oozing poison. He was crying out in pain constantly. Toromillo tired of his crying and put a bullet through his head. It was merciful, in a way. The scorpion bite would have killed him within the next few hours anyway.

Toromillo decided to make the most of the dead man's body. He wrote out in long hand his series of "demands" and attached them to the man's clothing:

1. We demand justice for the poorest of the poor in Colombia!
2. We demand an end to American aid to the Colombian army!
3. We demand an immediate end to extradition!
4. We demand that the army withdraw from Vaupés!
5. We demand the immediate, unconditional release of all *FARC* hostages in government hands!

That night the hijackers dumped the man's body at a tiny crossroads store, then got out of there as fast as possible. It was their first communication with the outside world.

Chapter Fourteen

"Ana," her editor's voice pleaded over the phone, "you can't go meet that man! You put some of his best buddies in jail! He'll kidnap you, too, if he doesn't kill you first!"

"This is the biggest story of our lives," she said. "How can I not go?"

So it was that, despite the editor's pleas, Ana hired a taxi to take her to the predetermined spot in the jungle where Botero promised to meet her. When they arrived, the taxi driver was incredulous. "Here?" he asked. "You want to be let out here?"

Restrepo assured him she did.

"Do you want me to wait for you?" he asked, though he had no intention of actually waiting.

"No," she said. "I want you to get out of here as fast as you can."

She paid him and closed the door. He turned the cab around and roared back down the crude jungle road as fast as the potholes would let him. Once he was gone, the jungle was absolutely empty of human noise. The roar of insect voices, bird calls, and rustling leaves resumed again after the brief human interruption.

"This jungle must be the same today as it's been for ten thousand years," she said to herself.

A bit nervous but not afraid, she looked around for a place to sit. Nothing seemed inviting, so she stayed on her feet. In a minute or so, she heard a voice behind her. She turned to see a gray-haired man in a *FARC* colonel's uniform standing no more than five feet away from her.

Two things amazed her about him immediately. The first was that he could approach so close completely unseen. This was obviously a man who knew what he was doing. The second was that Ernesto Botero was almost the exact size, weight, coloring, and age as her own father.

After touring the wreckage in Dallas, the American President met the press. In his open statement, he laid out the evidence. First, he connected the attack in Dallas to Jorge Toromillo. The evidence was by that point indisputable. Then, pointedly, he connected Jorge Toromillo to the *FARC* and to the government of Venezuela.

"Because of this direct evidence, I am ordering the Attorney General to implement an immediate, complete trade embargo on Venezuela. I realize this will be costly for all of us as Americans," he said, looking around the room. "Venezuela is a major exporter of crude oil. But we as Americans cannot and will not tolerate actions like this from anyone. I ask you, my fellow Americans, to share this sacrifice until this matter can be resolved."

As soon as he finished, the press let loose with a barrage of questions. Petroleum futures markets in New York and London went crazy. President Perez, watching from his office in Caracas, felt like someone had just placed a noose around his neck.

"My God," he said to his aides. "My God, my God, my God…"

The situation in Caracas began to worsen from that moment. Much of the city was in open rebellion. Reports of uprisings in other cities were beginning to filter in. The CIA, at the President's order, initiated its long-prepared operational plan for bringing down the Perez government.

By the end of the second day, at least four armed groups were scouring the jungles for the kidnaped passengers: the Colombian army, the *FARC*, and separate special forces units from the United States and Venezuela.

Finding five separate groups of men in a place as forbidding as the Colombian Amazon makes finding a needle in a haystack child's play. As with the rest of the operation, Toromillo had planned this part of the action to the last detail.

Ernesto Botero stood alone with Ana Restrepo in the Vaupés jungle. "So, you are the writer who has caused us so many problems," he said.

"So you are the man who has torn my country to shreds," she replied.

Ana was nothing if not fearless. Nevertheless, she couldn't get over Botero's uncanny resemblance to her father, far away in Barranquilla.

Botero didn't show any emotion at her comment. Instead, he addressed her in a soft, almost fatherly tone. "*M'hija* (my daughter), sometimes our enemies are not who we think they are."

"Why did you want to see me?" she asked.

She could guess, but wanted to hear it from him.

"The *FARC* commanders ordered me to speak to you," he said. "We want you to know we had nothing to do with this."

"Am I supposed to believe that…just because you say it?" she questioned.

If she was going to be kidnaped or killed anyway, she might as well ask the questions on her heart. "You've been doing things like this for decades!"

"Yes, *m'hija*," he answered. "Which is why you can believe me when I say we didn't do this one. We have never attacked a target in the United States, though we have taken American hostages here in Colombia. This is an act of war against America. I assure you the *FARC* is not suicidal. One war at a time is enough for us."

"Then why have the attackers used your name and disappeared into your jungle," she demanded.

"Maybe someone is using our name to provoke a war, to serve their own purposes. There are people in the world who would do such things. Ask enough questions," he said, "and you'll find the answers."

Almost against her will, Restrepo found herself respecting this soft-spoken old warrior. They spent more than an hour talking. Ana had the sense that this man, like Miguel, was exactly what he seemed.

At the end of the time, Botero said, "Promise me, *m'hija*, you will tell your young friend Escalante about this conversation."

"How do you know about Escalante?" Ana asked, taken aback.

"He has been hunting me for months," he answered. "How can I not know about him? I know something else about him, too. Something you appreciate as well."

"What?," Ana asked.

"He believes in truth, not lies. For many people, blaming this tragedy on the *FARC* will be convenient. It will let them do what they've wanted to do for years. But it isn't true. Your friend Escalante will know the difference. If we have to fight," he said, "let's fight over what we believe to be true, not over what we know to be lies."

"Promise me you'll tell Escalante what I've told you," Botero concluded.

She nodded that she would.

"Well, then. It's time for us to go," he said.

Then, as if he were commanding thin air he said, "Take her back to town! Don't let anyone lay a hand on her."

At his word, five *FARC* commandos materialized from their hiding places, as if from nowhere. Ana was startled, but Botero put his hand on her arm to steady her.

"You have nothing to fear from these men. Not today, at least."

Chapter Fifteen

Don Evans had finished his work by early the next morning. The casualties had been airlifted out to the American carrier *Theodore Roosevelt*, on station in the southern Caribbean. Many Colombians were well aware of the irony of the *Roosevelt* battle group prowling off their coast. Theodore Roosevelt was the American President young Colombians were taught had stolen Panama from them to build his canal.

The rest of the released hostages, their statements taken and their health verified, climbed aboard the waiting C-130. The Marines escorted them across the tarmac, shielding their bodies from the surrounding Colombian military as if they expected a firefight to break out any minute. The plane lumbered down the runway and into the sky around three o'clock in the morning, heading for Dallas. This time the escorting planes were Marine F/A 18s from the *Roosevelt*. The Marine planes peeled off as the C-130 crossed back into American airspace.

The plane arrived shortly before noon at Dallas' big airport, DFW, rather than shattered Love Field. The President of the United States stood by to welcome them as they got off the plane. Don Evans walked up to the President and said, "Mission accomplished, sir."

"Good job, son," the President answered, choking back a tear.

He was relieved beyond words to see that so many of the passengers were not only accounted for, but seemed well and in decent spirits. His chief preoccupation now, of course, was the hostages. sweltering somewhere out there in the jungle.

Shortly before midnight, as four separate teams of commandos were searching for any sign of the hostages, the Venezuelan contingent came across the body of the murdered American. Toromillo had dumped it at a tiny crossroads, near a small Colombian *tienda* (store). To hide the scorpion sting, which was the true cause of death, Toromillo had hacked the body's left leg off below the knee.

The Venezuelans were cataloguing the gruesome scene and contacting their commanders when the American special forces detail arrived unseen. The Americans quickly formed a perimeter surrounding the Venezuelans. Once his men were in place, the American commander shouted at the Venezuelan troops to drop their weapons. He gave the command in English.

The Venezuelan soldiers pivoted in the direction of the order. The Americans, battle-hardened veterans of Afghanistan and Iraq, opened fire. Twenty seconds later, four Venezuelan commandos lay dead and two others mortally wounded. The others managed to escape into the dense undergrowth. None managed to get off a shot.

The Americans advanced cautiously onto the scene. Once they discovered the hostage's mangled body, they re-formed their perimeter facing outward and called for air support. Half an hour away by air in Mitú, a Marine Corps V-22 lifted vertically into the air, carrying a heavily-armed squadron and a medical team. A helicopter gun ship followed.

Both the Colombian army and *FARC* units in the area were drawn to the scene by the gunfire. They set up positions opposite each other, watching the Americans guarding the body. The *FARC* commandos considered launching an attack, but thought better of it. The Colombian army troops considered making contact with their erstwhile

American "allies," but also thought better of it. It was a pitch black night. No one was especially eager to die.

For the American troops waiting on the ground, air support seemed to take forever to arrive. Their night vision equipment told them they had company, not far off in the jungle. They kept their weapons loaded and ready. After what seemed like hours, they heard the sound of rotors in the night sky and were able to breathe again.

The gun ship commander's voice crackled over the radio to the commander on the ground. "We see bandits on two sides of your position. Do we take them out?"

The ground commander replied, "Negative. They seem to be staying put. Do not take them out."

At that, the two giant machines hovered directly above the men on the ground. Airborne, everyone realized they were sitting ducks for a rocket-propelled grenade round. The gunners on both ships kept their eyes focused for any kind of movement which might signal an attack. A voice rang out over the gun ship's loudspeaker, this time in Spanish, "We have your positions covered. Do not move! I repeat, do not move or we will fire!"

The army and *FARC* troops froze in place and remained as motionless as living human beings can. While they stayed still, the Marine combat team rappelled to the ground. Half of them reinforced the perimeter while the other half captured both of the unknown detachments outside it. The "prisoners" were herded into the light of the perimeter, where a gruff Marine major awaited them.

"Who the hell are you?" he demanded through an interpreter.

"32nd Commandos, 4th Division, Army of the Republic of Colombia," one replied.

"12th Detachment, *Frente 58, Fuerzas Armadas Revolucionarias de Colombia*," replied the other.

"Well, well, well," the Major grinned. "Old friends, no doubt."

Everyone stood silent a moment until a Marine Lance Corporal found Toromillo's letter attached to the dead American's body. He brought it to the Major. The Major read it, his face twisting with rage.

"Is this what you do to unarmed Americans?" he screamed at the *FARC* commander.

"No, señor," he answered. "This is not our…"

The Major cut him off. "You wanna try that shit on a fucking live American now, you son of a bitch?!"

He was so livid one of the Special Forces soldiers physically grabbed him to keep him from attacking the *FARC* commander with his bare hands. All the Marines started toward the captured guerrillas, murder in their eyes.

The American Special Forces commander intervened. "Stand down!" he ordered.

The Major took another step forward, struggling against the other soldier's grasp. The commander barked again, "Stand down, goddamn it! That's an order!"

This time the Marines obeyed.

"We've got more important things to do, Major. We've got to find the others." Turning to the Colombian army commander, he said in Spanish, "Do you have any idea where they might be?"

"We think they're moving south and east toward the border," the commander replied.

"Well," the Special Forces commander replied, "let's get these bodies out of here and see if we can find 'em."

The Marines hoisted the body of the dead American and the identification papers of the slain Venezuelan troops to the helicopters above.

"Fuckin' Venezuelans," one of them spat when he saw the IDs. "Too bad we couldn't have killed more of the bastards."

Absent a landing site, there was no practical way to hoist the *FARC* prisoners into the choppers. Instead they left them bound and gagged, guarded by three Colombian soldiers, and radioed for the Colombian army to get them. After that the Americans, Marine and Special Forces, headed out with the Colombians toward the southeast.

Toromillo, however, wasn't headed southeast. After his team had dumped the American's body, all five teams doubled back toward the northwest, moving toward central Vaupés. With each passing moment, though, the hostages were becoming less useful. The atrocities had already been committed.

"If we haven't pissed the Americans off yet," Toromillo said to himself, "it can't be done."

Toromillo was sure by around four in the morning that someone—guerrilla, soldier, American, or Venezuelan—had found the body he'd left behind. The so-called *FARC* demands would have been communicated, one way or the other. He would leave another hostage behind as bait.

To that end, one of his teams took Congressman Cook to a clearing in the forest, pushed him in the direction of the nearest town, and let him go. He was instructed to tell the American authorities that the hostages would be released in exchange for $18,000,000, a cool million per head.

Toromillo took the other eighteen hostages four hours further into the jungle, blindfolded them, and stood them in line like he was going to shoot them all. Then he and the hijackers disappeared silently into the underbrush. The hostages stood like statues, awaiting the death shots.

Southwest Captain Newman was the first to free an eye from the blindfold and realize their lives had been spared. In the murky morning light of the jungle, he and the other hostages freed themselves from their bonds. Almost as one they sank to their knees in the most heartfelt prayer of thanks any of them had ever uttered. They were lost in the jungle. They had no idea which direction to go or what lay around the next tree. But they were free. For the moment, that was all that mattered.

Hernan Virrey's name first surfaced in news accounts shortly before noon that day. Another "anonymous State Department source" leaked him as the "Colombian hero who tried to warn us." Predictably, Virrey was besieged by reporters within hours.

The international media arrived like a great storm through the single strip airport outside the city of Armenia, in the middle of Colombia's richest coffee-growing zone. They made their way through winding mountain roads lined with banana, yucca, and coffee fields to the Virrey plantation, nestled in the foothills of the *Cordillera Central*, the branch of the Andes mountains parting the heart of the country.

Virrey's estate was stunning. The main house, about half a mile off the road, was surrounded by a tall, whitewashed security wall. Virrey instructed his staff let all the reporters in and treat them well. Inside the beautiful, white, Spanish colonial *hacienda* overlooking the entire lush valley, the reporters found an elaborate lunch and an open bar awaiting them.

Virrey himself turned out to be a congenial hero: immaculately well-dressed, graying slightly, speaking perfect, Texas-accented English. He had earned an Agronomy degree at Texas Tech University, he told them. Neither the CIA nor the various news agencies had turned up anything to suggest that Virrey was other than what he seemed—a wealthy, well-connected coffee-grower from Quindía Province.

"Why did you release this information?" one reported asked.

"Of course, sir," Virrey answered, "I did it in hopes of saving innocent lives."

"How did you find out about Jorge Toromillo?" another grilled.

"There is a strong coffee growers' collective here in Colombia," he said. "We are always alert to anything that might harm our country's interests. We have had our eyes on Mr. Toromillo for a long time."

"Do you believe the Venezuelans are behind this?" asked a reporter from Dallas.

"That's a question for the governments involved to sort out," Virrey said.

Noting the reporter's Dallas accreditation, he added, "Let me express my deepest sorrow to the people of a State I love, a State I once called home—Texas."

Chapter Sixteen

By that time, word of the midnight clash between US and Venezuelan troops in the Colombian jungles was being broadcast worldwide. Details emerged fairly quickly. CNN led its report by saying, "Last night in the jungles of southeast Colombian, an American Special Forces unit surprised a Venezuelan unit which had apparently just killed one the Southwest hostages. In an exchange of gunfire, six Venezuelans were killed and the body of the hostage recovered.

"Shortly thereafter, aided by helicopter gun ships and a rapid response combat team from the US Marine Corps, American and Colombian troops captured a detachment of *FARC* guerrillas in the same vicinity.

"Troops found a letter in the dead hostage's clothing stating the hijackers' demands:

1. We demand justice for the poorest of the poor in Colombia!
2. We demand an end to American aid to the Colombian army!
3. We demand an immediate end to extradition!
4. We demand that the army withdraw from Vaupés State!
5. We demand the immediate, unconditional release of all *FARC* hostages in government hands!

"This document and last night's combat seem to confirm the direct involvement of both the Venezuelan government and the *FARC* guerrilla army in the terrorist assault on Dallas last week."

Watching the news in his Caracas office, Venezuelan President Perez became violently ill. When he had recovered somewhat, his police commander hesitantly told him that large units of both the military and National Police seemed to be melting away. "What about the Presidential Guard," Perez asked him.

"They are still with us," the commander said. "1ˢᵗ Battalion is still in its barracks and 2ⁿᵈ Battalion is guarding the information centers of the government."

"Have we been able to make contact with the Americans yet?" Perez asked the Foreign Minister.

"Not substantively, sir. They are still 'evaluating.'"

"Blessed Virgin Mother!" the President sighed.

By mid-afternoon, the United States and Colombia had both recalled their Ambassadors from Caracas. The American State Department warned all US citizens in the country to get out as quickly as possible, citing "deteriorating conditions."

President Perez went before reporters to assure Americans that they were safe in his country. He denounced the terror attack in Dallas and stressed that Venezuela had nothing to do with it.

An obviously angry Fox News reporter asked, "How do you explain the killing of an American hostage by Venezuelan troops?"

Perez himself bristled, "There is no proof whatsoever that they harmed the man. The United States should explain why it killed six of our soldiers without provocation in Colombia."

"What were your troops doing in Colombia to start with?" a Colombian journalist demanded.

"Our troops were there to assist the Colombians in finding the hostages," Perez shouted, his face reddening.

At that point, his aides hustled him out of the room.

Within an hour, the American Department of Defense released ballistics reports matching the bullet in the body of the dead hostage with the standard issue Venezuelan military sidearm. A Colombian government spokesman told the international press, "At no time did the government of Colombia request help from the government of Venezuela. Any Venezuelan troops in our country were there illegally."

The Americans upped the pressure late that afternoon, ordering the aircraft carrier *USS Abraham Lincoln* to station off Colombia's Pacific coast. This doubled the American military power in striking distance of both the *FARC*'s strongholds in Colombia and of Venezuela itself. A United Nations spokesman, while condemning the terrorist attacks and the loss of innocent lives, called predictably for restraint.

Ana Restrepo's cell phone rang again as she sat by Miguel Escalante's hospital bed in Bogotá. Escalante was awake and in pain. He had suffered a concussion and multiple fractures. The doctors told Ana they thought he would recover fully, given enough time and rest.

"*M'hija,*" the familiar voice said over the phone. Colombian fathers often addressed their daughters this way.

"Señor Botero," she answered.

"This man Virrey is not what he seems," Botero said.

"Again I have to ask why I should believe you," Restrepo replied.

"One reason, *m'hija*, is simply that you are there and not here."

Restrepo grasped the point without explanation. By letting her go, Botero passed up a delicious opportunity to avenge the *FARC* on one of its harshest media critics. It had avenged itself on journalists hundreds of times in the past.

"May I speak to Captain Escalante?" he asked.

"How did you know I was with him," Restrepo blurted out, genuinely shocked.

Of course, the *FARC* had its spies all over Colombia, but even in a military hospital in the capital? Botero said nothing, but only laughed quietly. Ana handed the phone to Escalante.

"If I heard your voice under any other circumstances," Escalante said, "I would put a bullet through your head."

"Likewise, *amigo*," Botero answered.

"There is one thing and one thing only you have to know, Captain. I know you will respect this, because you know I would not have released your lady friend under any other circumstances. We had nothing to do with this attack or these hostages. The world may not believe us, but you are a man who respects the truth. Look deeply enough into your Señor Virrey and you will find he is not what he seems to be. That is the truth."

With that Botero hung up the phone and disappeared into the mists in Vaupés. Escalante and Restrepo, lives joined even closer together now by a common tragedy, held hands in silence in the hospital room, watching the crisis unfold on the news.

Congressman James Cook, Republican of Texas, appeared in the doorway of a tribal *cacique* (chieftain) in the heart of the Colombian jungle about dawn. His clothes were torn and bloody from the ordeal, his pale skin mottled from heat and insect bites. The *cacique* was in another village at that particular moment.

The *cacique*'s family spoke no English. Cook, of course, spoke only English. There was no denying his distress, though, so the *cacique*'s wife and daughters, together with the women of the village, did what Colombian women do almost instinctively: they put themselves to great trouble to make him comfortable.

Using hand gestures, they convinced him first to sit down. Then they brought him coffee and a breakfast of rice and fried plantain. Cook ate it ravenously, the first food he'd had since his last meal in Dallas. When he had finally relaxed a little, the women coaxed him into removing his shirt and began treating the wounds on his arms and head.

When he realized they intended to help him and not harm him, the rough, tough Congressman from Texas dissolved in tears of exhaustion and relief. His caretakers understood the emotion, even if they had no idea who this strange white man was or why he had wandered into their midst.

By the time the *cacique* returned from the neighboring village at midday, Cook was sound asleep in the *cacique*'s own cot. The women had washed his clothes by hand and hung them carefully to dry beside him. All his remaining possessions were stacked there as well, watched over ferociously by the eldest daughter of the house.

The *cacique* made as if to wake him. His wife absolutely forbade it. "Send for the *soldados*, (soldiers)" she said. "Let this poor man sleep."

The *soldados* who came were from the *FARC*. They immediately recognized him as one of the hostages and sent word up the chain of command. So it was that Ernesto Botero, lifelong communist revolutionary, came face to face with James Cook, lifelong capitalist and bulwark of the American right-wing.

Botero brought along a *FARC* doctor, who examined Cook from top to bottom. His head was swollen from being whacked by Toromillo's gun the day before. But his cuts and bruises had been well tended by the native medicines. "My major concern," the doctor said, "is yellow fever and malaria. This man has been without protection in the jungle for a day and half."

"Will the yellow fever vaccination do him any good at this point?" Botero asked.

"It won't hurt," the doctor replied.

He pulled the syringe and vial out of his medical bag. Cook stiffened with fear.

"Don't hurt me anymore!" he cried in English.

To Cook's great surprise, Botero answered him in English. "This is a vaccination, sir. It's to prevent you from coming down with yellow fever."

Cook was immensely relieved to hear an English-speaking voice. "Who are you?" he asked.

"I am Colonel Ernesto Botero of the Revolutionary Armed Forces of Colombia," he replied.

"The…the *FARC*?" Cook asked, fearfully.

"Yes, the *FARC*," Botero replied.

"Am I a prisoner?" Cook asked again.

"You are not, sir. It is my responsibility to escort you safely to the Colombian government."

Chapter Seventeen

Somewhere in south-central Vaupés, the surviving American hostages were trying to find a way out of the jungle. Captain David Newman's long-ago survival training in the US Navy was coming in handy, but the physical and emotional exhaustion of the entire group was weighing heavily.

Newman knew that if he could climb up into the jungle canopy far enough to see the sun, he would be able to tell which direction was which. He also knew that neither he nor anyone else in the group had the strength at this point to do so. The midday heat and humidity were fierce, sapping what little strength the men had left. Newman and a few others begin looking around for something suitable to eat.

Ernesto Botero and his *FARC* detachment were nearing Mitú, with Congressman Cook in tow. Botero and his troops hadn't slept in thirty-six hours.

Cook plied Botero with question after question during the long journey through the jungle. "How long had he been in the *FARC*? Why did the *FARC* target Americans? What was the connection between the *FARC* and Venezuela?"

Botero had answered each question as honestly as he could. He could tell Cook didn't believe a word of it, though. You can't persuade someone whose mind is already made up, Botero thought to himself.

Half a mile from the nearest Colombian army outpost, Botero and his men released the Congressman, unharmed. It was the second time that very long day, someone had pushed Cook into a clearing and let him go.

He walked anxiously up the jungle path, not knowing what lay ahead. The cries of birds and the whirring of insects echoed inside his ears. He felt the hairs on the back of his neck standing on end.

Suddenly there were shouts in Spanish and the sound of running feet. In an instant, he was surrounded by armed Colombian soldiers, all looking at him like he'd stepped off a visiting spaceship. The sight of a pale, white, middle-aged man dressed in a *cacique*'s robe, carrying his own neatly-folded clothes in a crudely woven banana leaf bag, was not everyday occurrence in Vaupés.

Don Evans, feeling more and more like a hero, picked up the secure line to inform the Secretary of State in Dallas that Congressman Cook was safe. "Rescued by the Colombian army," he said.

In their brief conversation, Evans had gleaned from what he took to be Cook's delirium that he had been in the custody of the *FARC* until shortly before his rescue.

"Apparently," Evans told Washington, "they stripped him out of his clothes and were trying to hide him with some Indians out in the jungle."

Evans paused, listening to the voice on the other line. He then said into the phone, "Yes ma'am, that just about seals it."

Another pause. "No, unfortunately we haven't been able to find the other hostages. From what we've seen and heard, though, I'm afraid we don't have much reason for hope."

Ana Restrepo set aside the entire evening to spend with Miguel Escalante in the hospital. As the sun began to set, Miguel's headache returned with a vengeance. Ana summoned the nurse, who gave him a shot for the pain.

When the nurse left, Restrepo crawled up into the hospital bed beside him. "Ana," he said groggily, "you don't have to stay."

"I know I don't," she said.

She gently pulled his head to rest on her chest, stroking his hair with her fingers.

Fifteen minutes later Escalante snored gently in her embrace. Both of them were startled by a commotion in the hall. Miguel's military instincts took over and he tried to struggle to his feet. The conversation with Botero had unnerved him. Despite Miguel's best efforts, though, he couldn't get out of bed.

Instead, the door opened and Vicente Arena, President of Colombia, walked into the room.

"Relax, Captain. I'm not the enemy," the President said.

Escalante collapsed back onto Ana's shoulder.

"Señorita Restrepo," the President said with a fond smile. They had spoken to each other often since Arena became President. "As always, a great pleasure!"

"Please forgive me for not getting up, Mr. President," she said.

"Of course," he replied. "Stay right where you are. Is there anything you need, Captain? You seem to be the only bright spot for our country in this terrible event."

Escalante shook his head weakly. "No, Mr. President. I let them take the passengers away. They were right under my nose."

"No, Captain," Arena said, "you did everything you could, above and beyond what anyone could expect. Don't blame yourself."

Arena stepped around to Escalante's bedside, checking the younger man's forehead for fever as if he were his own father.

"There is one thing," Escalante said groggily.

He was exhausted and the pain medication was making its presence felt.

"Miguel," Ana warned, "I won't let you wear yourself out."

"She's right," Arena said. "Listen to her."

Escalante painfully pulled himself to a sitting position and said, "No, Mr. President. This affects her too."

Arena said, "What is it, then?"

He motioned for his chief of staff to take notes.

"Tell him about Botero," Escalante said to Ana.

"I will tell him, Miguel. But not here."

Ana unwound herself from Escalante's exhausted embrace. Arena helped him lie back on the bed and carefully tucked the covers in around him. He and Ana went out into the hall.

"What about Botero," Arena said.

"He met me in the jungle, outside Mitú," Ana said.

Arena was incredulous. "How did he find you? It's a miracle you're still alive!"

"I went to him," Restrepo answered.

"What on earth for?" the President asked, shocked that a journalist would take such a foolish risk.

"He guaranteed my safety."

"What did he tell you?"

Ana replied, "He told me the *FARC* had nothing to do with this."

"Well, of course he would say that," Arena's chief of staff broke in.

"But he called me…here…tonight," she added. "He spoke to Miguel."

"My God! He called you here, in a military hospital? No wonder the Captain tried to get up." Arena said. "What did he tell you?"

"He told me again that the *FARC* had nothing to do with this and that Hernan Virrey is not what he seems."

"Why on earth would anyone believe him," Arena asked.

"He said the proof in what he was saying is that I am here and not there," Ana replied.

The point was not lost on the President. He thought for a moment. "Well, thank God you weren't kidnaped. It's out of character for them not to have taken you."

The chief of staff broke in again, "Then again, they have a lot to fear these days. They may be trying to throw us off their tracks."

"Yes," Ana said. "But he may be telling us the truth."

After Ana finished, President Arena sent her back into the room. "Take care of Escalante," he ordered. "He's a hero."

"I will, Mr. President," she smiled.

When she was gone, Arena turned to his chief of staff. "If Botero is right, then what are we looking at here?"

The chief of staff shook his head. "I don't know."

Arena turned the possibilities over in his mind. "I believe the Americans will attack, regardless of what we say," he said, thinking aloud.

"Well," the chief answered, "that will solve our *FARC* problem for us."

"It might," Arena said. "But it will bring the elephants into our country in a way we've never had them before, too."

"Isn't that a small price to pay?" asked the chief. "We haven't been able to win this war on our own."

Arena was above all a patriot. He grimaced at the thought of someone else winning the war for them.

"The Americans are convinced Venezuela is behind this, too," Arena continued. "They've been looking for a way to get rid of Perez for awhile now. This will surely make that happen."

"Again," the chief added, "that's good for us. We've known for years that Perez and the *FARC* are in bed with each other."

"The question," Arena said, "is what will happen after? If Perez goes, what happens in Venezuela? Who benefits? If we win the war with the *FARC* too soon, what happens here? Who wins if there is anarchy in both countries?"

"Other than the anarchy part, aren't those the things you've spent the last six years trying to accomplish?" the chief of staff asked him.

"Yes, no doubt. But if things change too far, too fast, we won't be able to control it. How do we integrate the guerrillas back into society when this is over?" Arena asked, seeing the dilemma. "And if we win too fast, how do we demobilize our own soldiers without crashing the economy?"

The two men stood there in silence a moment.

"If Botero wasn't lying," Arena said, shaking his head with disgust, "I wonder what in the hell is going on here?"

Chapter Eighteen

The Venezuelan cabinet stayed in session in its emergency bunker throughout the night. The situation on the street was deteriorating rapidly. Army units close to the capital refused orders to move in. An enormous crowd chanted anti-Perez slogans on the plaza in front of the Presidential Palace, half a mile from the bunker where Perez and his officials were gathered.

The news coverage was uniformly bad. No one, it seemed, believed a word of the Perez government's many denials. The circumstantial evidence was too strong: an identifiable Venezuelan intelligence agent had commanded the attack. Venezuelan soldiers seemed to be responsible for the death of one of the hostages. Then, of course, there were endless replays of Perez himself saying to the American Secretary of State, "Don't mess with me, madam. I bite."

"God, if I could take those words back..." Perez exclaimed. "Can't those people see this is all smoke and mirrors? Are they incapable of rational thought? Why on earth would I provoke a war with the United States?"

Perez's military chiefs kept him advised of the American battle fleets in both the Caribbean and the Pacific. He didn't really need them to, since CNN was thoughtfully providing live coverage of America's military preparations. All night long his Foreign Minister tried to get through to the American Secretary of State.

He had called the British, the Russians, the Germans, even the French. None was willing to help. "Not even the goddamn French," Perez sighed.

Finally, at 4:30 in the morning, the Foreign Minister got through to the Secretary of State. Perez and his cabinet felt a huge relief as the woman's voice was finally patched through to the speaker-phone.

"Madam Secretary," Perez said, "how good to hear your voice!"

"We have a message for you, President Perez," she said, her voice like ice. "We bite too."

"Madam Secretary! Madam Secretary, please!" Perez shouted.

It was no use.

She had hung up.

At 5:30 in the morning, Caracas awakened to a series of shattering explosions. Four American cruise missiles targeted each of the main command and control centers in buildings housing the Venezuelan Army, Air Force, Ministry of Defense, and Intelligence. All four buildings essentially collapsed on themselves, decapitating the Perez government.

Precisely thirty seconds later, another barrage of four cruise missiles struck the main barracks compound of the Venezuelan Presidential Guard. The Guard had awakened like everyone else at the sound of the first strikes. They were groggily pulling on their uniforms when the second strike blasted them into the world to come.

Now militarily unprotected, cut off from any possible friendly support, Perez and his leading ministers sprinted from their bunker into a waiting Venezuelan Air Force helicopter. They had planned for this contingency many times, given the country's history of *coups*. They had not planned on the presence of an American stealth fighter over their capital, though.

The ungainly chopper lifted off, pulling up to make a run over the mountains into safety. The American pilot, unseen by radar below, locked in the target and spoke the word, "Fire," into the plane's computer. A brilliant yellow flame lit up the night sky as the missile roared toward its target. Seconds later, the missile struck the helicopter, triggering an immense midair explosion.

"We bite too, you son of a bitch!" the pilot said as he turned the plane around and headed for home.

The *FARC* in its jungle strongholds had more than enough firepower to hold out against the Colombian army. The Colombian army had long known where those strong points were, but lacked the air power to overcome them. The result had been a war neither side could win.

American intelligence, too, knew the locations of major *FARC* forces. Those locations had been programmed into the onboard systems of the giant B-52 bombers now lumbering down the runway from Barksdale Air Force Base in Louisiana. By midmorning they approached their targets, so high in the air those on the ground couldn't hear them coming.

The *FARC* had never faced a competent air force. It had only rudimentary radar and, thus, no effective warning. The last thing hundreds of *FARC* leaders and soldiers felt was the sudden heaving of the ground as the American bombs blasted their defensive positions into oblivion. The bombing continued around the clock five ferocious days.

The huge B-52s carpeted the *FARC*'s infrastructure and heavy weapons with high explosives. C-130s carrying enormous "daisy cutter" bombs dropped them on *FARC* troop concentrations, reducing dozens of acres to burned-out stubble with each blast. Smaller attack planes carried out pinpoint strikes on particular targets. By the time it ended, American commanders estimated 75% of the *FARC* positions throughout the country had been destroyed.

In vast areas of the jungle, though, nothing moved at all after the bombing. Survivors stumbled through an eery, desolate silence where days before the sounds of nature were everywhere. Those who did not live through it simply couldn't imagine it.

The Americans did not consult the Colombian military in advance. No permission was either asked or given. They simply warned Arena to move his troops out of range. When the US commanders were confident they had fatally wounded the *FARC*, they ended the bombing.

Then and only then did they inform Arena. Arena did the one thing he could do. He ordered the army in to mop up the remnants.

Ernesto Botero died under the bombs as he lived, a dedicated communist revolutionary to the end.

The released hostages were at least a hundred miles away from the nearest *FARC* emplacement when the horrific American bombardment began. Like everyone else in eastern Vaupés, they felt and heard it loud and clear despite the distance. Most of the hostages were beyond help by that point, overwhelmed by the ravages of the jungle..

The few still able-bodied pulled themselves together and walked in the direction of the explosions. Captain Newman, fighting against the intense flashes of fever that engulfed his body every few minutes, had no real idea of how long or how far they had walked when a Colombian patrol discovered them.

Five of eighteen, Newman among them, were carried by the Colombian army back to civilization. A search party sent after the rest discovered five more alive on the ground. Two of them died shortly after being rescued.

Don Evans, after interviewing the delirious Captain Newman in the hospital, reported to his superiors that the American bombing had forced the *FARC* to release its hostages.

Miguel Escalante watched events unfold on TV from his hospital bed. He regretted bitterly being unable to participate in the final assault. He kept remembering his mother's death as the *FARC* was destroyed by others.

Ana Restrepo, by his side, tried to keep him calm.

Epilogue

Two months after the bombing of Colombia, a humble Foreign Service Officer was singled out as a hero during the President's State of the Union Address. "One fine man sitting in the Gallery tonight," the President told the nation, "exemplifies all that is best about public service in the United States of America. That man is Don Evans."

Ana Restrepo took a day away from tending to her new fiancé, Miguel Escalante, to interview Hernan Virrey in his marvelous *hacienda* in Quindía. Virrey had expected more of the same hero-worshiping press coverage he had received from practically every other media outlet in the world. Ana disappointed his expectations.

Restrepo had done her usual thorough work prior to the interview. *Don* Hernan, it turned out, had extensive holdings in Putumayo, in the extreme south of Colombia. According to information she had gleaned from an official at the American Drug Enforcement Agency, that region produced a particularly high grade of cocaine now making its way to the United States and Europe through new smuggling routes in Venezuela. The American agent admitted that one of the unintended consequences of the collapse of the Perez regime was a new *laissez faire* attitude among many in the Venezuelan military toward drug smuggling.

Throughout their interview, Virrey never lost his chivalrous demeanor or his cool. Nor did he give in to Ana's well-practiced charms. There was no alcohol, no seduction, no rohypnol.

Hernan Virrey saw himself, not without justification, as the conqueror of Colombia. He had accomplished everything he set out to. True to his predictions, the fools didn't even know it had happened. King Hernan submitted to no one's control but his own.

He denied every single one of Restrepo's "insinuations," as he called them.

Finally he said to her, "What do you want me to say, Ms. Restrepo? That I am a drug trafficker? That I am a friend of Jorge Toromillo? That somehow this was all a plot to kill Americans, bring down Perez, and destroy the *FARC*?

"What sane person would believe such things?" he concluded.

Venezuela's civil institutions struggled to recover from the demise of President Perez. Though the bombing had been mercifully short, nightmarish revenge followed. Perez's old enemies hauled hundreds and hundreds of his supporters out into the jungles, never to be heard from again.

The economic damage inflicted by years of tension and, ultimately, war with the United States, could not be repaired in a hurry. *Petroleos de Venezuela* had experienced the loss of thousands and thousands of experienced engineers. The American embargo on new technologies had bitten Venezuela's aging industry fiercely. What was left of PDV found it harder and harder to bring Venezuela's heavy crude to market.

Higher production costs and lower actual output had impacts around the globe. Yet in Venezuela the impact was by far the worst. Rates of poverty and infant mortality jumped as the modest public health gains of the Perez era collapsed.

The military government that replaced Perez was initially greeted with wild enthusiasm. Soon, though, its corruption and ineptitude became obvious. Larger and larger areas of the country became lawless, leading some in Western governments to question whether Venezuela would head down the same chaotic road as Colombia.

The jungle recovers quickly. Within a few months of the ferocious American bombing, the scarred remains of *FARC* strongholds were already beginning to give way to the creepers and vines. The Colombian government, with an absolute upper hand now, imposed a peace settlement on both the remnants of the *FARC* and on the *ELN*, Colombia's second largest rebel group.

The long war had resulted in literally millions of what the United Nations called "internally-displaced peoples," refugees. The process of getting these people out of the cities and back into their rural homes was hopelessly complex, far beyond the government's competence.

The demobilized guerrillas faced great challenges integrating back into the society. Adding to the strain, the Colombian security services began to demobilize. This twofold surge of the young and unemployed led to crime waves and unrest throughout the country's major cities.

It proved easier to win the war with American air power than to secure the peace.

The wedding of Ana Restrepo and Miguel Escalante took place six months later in the National Cathedral itself, on the *Plaza de Bolivar* in the center of Bogotá. Miguel had recovered enough to walk with only a modest amount of pain.

President Vicente Arena was the best man to this brightest of Colombian military heros. He whispered to Miguel as Ana walked down the aisle, "She is the most beautiful woman I have ever seen in my life."

Miguel agreed.

Don Evans, the newly appointed Ambassador of the United States of America to Colombia, seemed as always a bit awkward. Perhaps it was the formal attire, those around him said. After all, Evans had made his reputation in the jungle. No doubt, they said, he would seem more heroic, less out of place, if they saw him there. Nevertheless, at the appropriate moment he raised his glass on behalf of the American people to toast the newlyweds.

"*Salud!*" the crowd shouted at the top of its lungs.

Later President Arena stood up to offer a toast. As soon as he stood, the room fell silent. "I would like to offer a toast, not simply to two of the finest, most brilliant people our country has produced, but to our country itself. To Colombia!" he said. "To *our* Colombia!"

The crowd thundered its approval.

Far away, on an ornate balcony in an immense private estate overlooking a beach in the south of France, Jorge Toromillo sat alone sipping his morning coffee. It was rich and pungent.

Toromillo laughed quietly to himself. His new bank statement had arrived. More money poured into his numbered account each month than he could spend in ten years, even on the French Riviera. Business back home was good indeed.

A long, sleek yacht passed through the harbor buoys below. In the distance he heard the mournful bellow of a ship's whistle and the pleasant chatter of bird song. Toromillo loved watching the sea from his villa. For the first time in a long, long time, he felt content. His life's ambition was never to set foot in a jungle again.

He thought back on what he'd heard his countrymen say so often. "Tell them Colombia is not all about drugs," he repeated sarcastically.

"We also make a hell of a cup of coffee."

THE END

978-0-595-40800-9
0-595-40800-1

Printed in the United States
59240LVS00002B/220-381